Jonathan Aycliffe was born in Belfast in 1949. He studied English, Persian, Arabic and Islamic studies at the universities of Dublin, Edinburgh and Cambridge, and lectured at the universities of Fez in Morocco and Newcastle upon Tyne. The author of nine full-length ghost stories, he lives in the north of England with his wife. He also writes as Daniel Easterman, under which name he has penned several bestselling thrillers.

17. 12. 13.
4 7 14

THE SILENCE OF GHOSTS

GHOSTS

Jonathan Aycliffe

corsair

Constable & Robinson Ltd
55–56 Russell Square
London WC1B 4HP
www.constablerobinson.com

First published in the UK by Corsair
an imprint of Constable & Robinson Ltd, 2013

A copy of the British Library Cataloguing in
Publication Data is available from the British Library.

ISBN: 978-1-47210-512-7 (paperback)
ISBN: 978-1-47210-906-4 (ebook)

Typeset by TW Typesetting, Plymouth, Devon

Printed in the UK

1 3 5 7 9 10 8 6 4 2

For Beth, my blithe spirit, yet never silent, with love

The Ullswater Diaries of Dominic Lancaster RN: An Introduction

I hope you have a strong stomach, at least a stronger one than mine. The following pages do not make easy reading, and although I have done no more than edit them, I would not willingly return to them. And when at last you come to the end of them, I think you too may have no wish to set eyes on them again. For all that, I have published them in an attempt to set the record straight and to allow my grandfather an opportunity to speak out of the grave, to set the events of seventy years ago before the eyes of a younger generation. Looking again at what I have just written, I fancy I have mixed my metaphors. It is not a strong stomach you will need, but rather, strong nerves. There is little of the gory in what follows. No blood to speak of, nothing grisly, nothing blood-curdling. Yet, I urge you not to read the diaries by a dim light in darkness, or in those unsettled hours when the sun sets or the white moon rises over the moving sea, or when there is music in bewildered places, when you are alone and the cat scratches at the door.

What you have in front of you are wartime diaries kept by my late grandfather Dominic Lancaster, who died at the age of ninety-two in a long white bed at the Eden Valley Hospice just outside Carlisle. He died in some discomfort from tuberculosis. The disease had lain dormant in his lungs since the Second

World War, or so his doctors told him. How they could tell, I really don't know. Of course, as you will see for yourself when you read his account of things, TB wasn't the only thing he brought with him out of the conflict.

What really killed him, in my opinion, was the death of my grandmother Rose seven months earlier. She had kept him going all those years, she had been there to whisper soothing words when he woke at night screaming, in a cold sweat, when he came to her in the middle of the day, trembling because he had seen something in the garden or round a corner of the house. He clung to her, and I believe he spoke to her, told her his secrets when he would divulge none of them to the rest of us. As a child, I loved Rose more than I loved my own mother. Even my father liked her, and he liked nobody, least of all my grandfather.

When he died, I became his sole heir. The port importing business and the family house in London's Bedford Square passed to me rather than to my father, who was ill and had retired some years earlier. He had moved to Cornwall, to an old fisherman's house in St Ives. My mother had returned to France after their divorce, and I saw little of them both. I inherited the summer house on St Bees Head in Cumbria, where my grandfather and his beloved Rose had spent their later years together. And I was given charge of another house, one of which neither Dominic nor Rose had ever spoken to me. It was not mentioned in grandfather's will, but our lawyers found it in a separate, older document, and by legal calculation they decreed that it fell to me by default, as my father knew nothing of it either. I had no aunts or uncles who might have shed light on this, and at first I thought little of it. It cannot, I thought, have been of much importance, perhaps it was little more than a fancy hut tricked out for holiday visits spaced out by great gaps as the years passed, and wholly neglected in the end. Later, I was to know better.

Later I was to read my grandfather's trembling record of the time he had spent there, unsuspecting.

According to the will, this house was situated in the Lake District, on the shores of Ullswater, half in the beech trees and oaks of Hallinhag Wood and half by the path that leads from St Peter's Church in Martindale to Sandwick Bay. A letter accompanied the will, in which it was explained that this dwelling was called Hallinhag House and that it had been in the family since long before my grandfather's time. The letter added that it was my grandfather's dearest wish that I should see to its demolition. This was, he said, something that should have been done long ago, but for some reason he could not accomplish it in his lifetime. The house, he wrote, was not fit to live in.

It puzzled me that we had never visited it when I was growing up, even though it was not situated at a very great distance from my grandparents' holiday home on St Bees Head, a place we often visited. Nor had my father or mother spoken even once of it, nor my grandfather or grandmother ever let me know of its existence. It was not until I read his diaries that I understood better why Dominic had remained silent.

As a boy I had known my grandfather well. My father was often away on business, and my mother was greatly involved with her political work, so it often fell to my grandfather and grandmother to take their places. They lived in London then, as our family had done since the eighteenth century, and for many years he was Chief Executive of the Lancaster port importing business. He took the firm over during the Second World War, and brought Lancaster Port House through those lean and difficult years. My father took over when grandfather retired in his late sixties. He, Grandmother Rose and I often travelled to the Lakes together, though never to Ullswater. Our lakes were, in the main, Coniston Water and Windermere, not far from Ullswater. Looking back, I see that he avoided Ullswater deliberately. I once asked him where Wordsworth had seen his daffodils, and he professed not to know, for all that he read the poet regularly and knew everything about his life. The daffodils were on Gowbarrow Fell, about four miles from where Hallinhag House was situated. They grow there today in multitudes, as golden and dancing as ever, spreading among the trees with each spring that passes.

When the more complicated side of my inheritance had been sorted out – my grandfather's solicitor was an efficient yet kindly man who had dealt with our family for a great many years, just as his father and grandfather had done before him – I decided to pay a visit to my mysterious Ullswater house, filled with curiosity as to its size and condition. Despite the inheritance, money was short, and I was half inclined to ignore my grandfather's wishes if the house turned out to be viable. The Lakes were always popular with holidaymakers, especially the sort who wear woolly hats, lug heavy rucksacks up impossible slopes, and shove their tender feet into stout walking boots from Berghaus. I entertained hopes of a dwelling that I could put into a state of good repair and then rent or sell outright as a holiday home to some lucky family from London or Newcastle.

I arrived late one morning in September and stopped at Pooley Bridge, at the north end of the lake. There, I was given directions to head for the small village of Howtown, which I reached along a narrow country road that wound along the eastern shore. Ullswater appeared through the gaps in the trees – a grey, narrow lake hemmed in by undulating fells, with the mountains of the Helvellyn range to one side. They say it's the most beautiful lake in Britain, so I was keen to get on one of the famous steamers and go for a cruise. On its rippling waters the little boat forged its way bravely from Howtown to Pooley Bridge. Autumn lay on the lake like grey flannel, and a stiff wind threw sharp waves against the steamer's side.

I checked in at the ivy-covered Howtown Park Hotel, where I stayed to take lunch. Once I finished, I went to reception and asked a pretty young woman if she could direct me to Hallinhag House. She looked at me blankly and said she had never heard of a place by that name. Before I could read her the directions I'd taken from the solicitor's document, she murmured an apology and headed through a door that fell quietly shut behind her. When she returned two minutes later, she was accompanied by a much older man, who introduced himself as the hotel porter. He was frail-looking, with sallow skin and rheumy eyes, and I wondered how he had the strength to carry guests' luggage.

'My granddaughter tells me you're looking for a house here in Howtown,' he said, stretching out a bony hand to shake mine.

'Not quite in Howtown,' I corrected him. 'It's in the woods between here and somewhere called Hallinhag. That's where the house gets its name from, Hallinhag House. It belongs to my family, the Lancasters.'

I was about to explain things further, but one look at the old man's face stopped me in my tracks. It was as if he'd seen a ghost or as though my family name had aroused in him an unpleasant memory or a cause for deep revulsion. Nobody had ever looked at me in that way before.

'What is it?' I asked. 'You look upset. Have I said something wrong?'

He turned to his granddaughter. I could see that she too had been struck by the rapid change in his demeanour.

'Grandfather,' she said, 'whatever's up? The gentleman only asked where his house is. He's asking directions, that's all. Are you feeling all right?'

'Fine,' he snapped, 'I'm fine. Never felt better. But I'll be more myself once I get out of here. I'd thought that wretched place long forgotten.'

He looked at me again.

'And it was forgotten until you mentioned it just now. Just what do you plan to do with it?'

His abruptness took me aback, but I squared up to him.

'It's really none of your business,' I replied, 'but since you're in such a state about it, you may as well know that I'm thinking of turning it into a holiday cottage for myself, or I might sell it to someone looking for a Lakeland home. But I haven't seen it yet. Perhaps you can think of a more urgent use for it.'

He went on looking at me, the anger in his eyes clear to see.

'Have it knocked down, sir, what there is left of it. If you can find anyone willing to do the job, that is, for no one from Howtown or Pooley Bridge will touch it. It should have been knocked down years ago, sir. Now, if you'll excuse my rudeness, I have to get back to my chores. I'm sorry I can't be of further help to you.'

With which he turned and went back through the door he'd come in by. The young woman watched him go, her eyes wide and her mouth gaping. I could see she was genuinely upset, but I said nothing more of her grandfather's behaviour.

'Please don't mind him, sir,' she said. 'He's an old man and he's getting a bit soft in the head. But he means no harm.'

I reassured her that the outburst had left me unaffected, but inwardly I was still shaking from its vehemence, from the implied warning his words had contained. I tried to shrug it off, but I was like a small child whistling in the dark. I could not cast off the sense that the old man's words had meant something quite concrete, if only I could divine what that something was.

The girl told me to wait, then rushed outside and came back

with a young man, evidently the hotel gardener. A stout young man, tall and heavily built, he seemed unlikely to be anything but level-headed, and when I asked him for directions, he did not hesitate to tell me how to find my house. But when he was done and stood at the door, about to return to his digging and hoeing, he screwed his eyes up like someone reaching a decision, and he looked hard at me as if I was a weed that resisted all attempts to kill it.

'Don't think to spend the night there,' he said, his voice strained. 'And be careful who you speak to.'

'Do you mean it's haunted?' I retorted. 'Is that what all this is about? Some story for Hallowe'en that you locals all think is true?'

'It's not my place to say, sir. We mostly gives it a wide berth. I couldn't say whether it's haunted or not. No one I know has ever set foot in the place.'

He stepped away from me again, taking lengthy strides. I saw him take up the long shafts of a wheelbarrow into which he had been heaping leaves. A dog followed him, then dashed forward to sniff eagerly at the contents of the barrow. It was a large Münsterländer, full of curiosity and drive, like others of the breed. I wondered if our gardener went hunting with him.

Thanking the receptionist for her initiative, I left alone, following the directions I'd just been given. The houses of Howtown fell away quickly. A gravel pathway led me to the lake side. Where it turned along the lake, the last houses disappeared and I was forced to work my way slowly through sturdy trees that bravely tried to bar my way. I recognized oaks and beeches, with birches dotted here and there among them.

In the end, Hallinhag House proved easy to find. I came to a large clearing in which stood a considerable stone-built house. It stood two storeys' high and was built on a platform

7

of grey stone that must have been taken from a nearby quarry. The house had been roofed in local slate, but I noticed that many of the tiles had fallen and that moss and sundry weeds had taken up residence across the gaps and even on the original slate itself.

For all that I had just come from bright daylight, the clearing in which I now stood was mired in gloom. I had come well prepared, since I'd guessed there would be neither heating nor lighting inside. I retrieved my large Maglite torch from its canvas bag and switched it on. A little brought down by my two conversations at the hotel, I felt my spirits lift as I held the torch high and watched the powerful beam shine on the façade of the building. Long and heavy, the Maglite was as much a weapon as a torch, and I felt sure that I could see off any intruders who might show up, perhaps locals aggrieved by my opening the house against their clear wishes.

The front door seemed to be locked at first. I cursed the solicitor for not having given me the key. But another glance told me that, key or no key, the door would be solidly jammed. I had no idea when anyone had last lived here, but I could see at once that it hadn't been for several decades. I stepped back a few feet and rushed at the door, crashing into it with my right shoulder. It groaned and stood its ground, so I stepped back further and ran at it harder. Suddenly it gave way, leaving me to stumble into a wide hallway that had been plunged in darkness for who could say how long. I let the torchlight roam in a circle, picking out a broad staircase that rose to a landing and then twisted to the left and disappeared into yet more darkness that lay beyond the reach of my torch.

The pervasive gloom, the thick layers of dust, the cobwebs hanging in festoons everywhere, the grimness caused by the absence of much external light, the grime on the few cracked window panes that were left, the ubiquitous patches of damp – all these led me to despair and to a growing conviction that I had made a mistake. Hallinhag House, I realized, was beyond repair, at least so far as my budget allowed. I had already moved into the family apartments in Bedford Square. But I doubted that the eventual sale of Hallinhag would realize sufficient funds to spend on what could prove to be a bottomless pit. Not just that, but I would be undertaking the repair of a house with a bad reputation, a haunted house, perhaps, a house where something terrible may have happened, a murder or a suicide. Or perhaps nothing at all. The house's reputation was very likely nothing more than the result of local gossip. Whatever the locals thought or said or insinuated, I was too much of a rationalist to listen to their fears. That was then, of course: I know better now.

Slowly, I explored the house, walking through a shifting pattern of light and dark, chased by shadows, dispelling them with blows of the long beam that sliced the gloom. Everywhere I went I was met by patches of ingrained damp and cobwebs, and in the torchlight I could see spiders as they scuttled away from me. I have to admit that I don't much like spiders: their presence was the most unpleasant aspect of my exploration.

To my great surprise, the rooms were still filled with furniture. Chairs, sofas, beds, tables, curtains – all stood or hung as though untouched since my grandfather had abandoned Hallinhag House. Not for the first time, I felt frustrated by the vow of silence he must have imposed on himself. Only he had known whatever stories belonged to these shadows, what events had happened around this furniture, who had sat in these chairs, bathed in this bathroom, slept in these beds, who had been born here, who had died here.

The furniture was, of course, ruined beyond measure. Mould

and fungus had wrought a terrible vengeance on the soft furnishings. What had been cushions on the sofas, and sheets and blankets and pillows on the beds, had been reduced to what was little more than slush. Nothing here could be retrieved.

I snapped shut the notebook in which I had planned to write a rough inventory, like an archaeologist making his initial survey of an ancient and once-splendid site. But there was almost nothing to inventorize. I doubted there was treasure here. I put the notebook in my pocket and started to leave, eager to get back outside again, where there would be birdsong and green light. But when I reached the landing, I saw standing at the foot of the stairs a girl of about ten dressed in what appeared to be homemade clothes. The clothes seemed a little out of date: a knitted pink cardigan over a blue skirt that reached to well below her knees, and red shoes with a strap across the top. She had long black hair. As I drew close, I saw that she had the most piercing, intense eyes I had ever seen. She gave me quite a start, I must admit, but I recovered quickly and continued down the stairs, smiling. I realized she must have stepped inside, seeing the front door more than half open.

'Hello,' I said, 'where on earth have you come from?'

She did not answer, but waited impassively until I reached the bottom of the stairs. When I did so and was standing only feet away from her, she flashed a warm, friendly smile.

'I'm Octavia,' she said. 'Perhaps you've heard of me.'

I shook my head and smiled.

'Afraid not,' I said. 'I'm not from these parts. But I'm sure we can be friends.'

I reached out a hand as if to shake hers, but she drew back a little, and I decided she must be shy.

'You must come from London,' she said. 'That's where I used to live. When I was deaf.'

I guessed she must have cochlear implants; there was no trace of any infirmity now. I knew a little about such matters. My grandfather had established a small school for the deaf in Bloomsbury. That was before my day. Was this pure coincidence? I wondered. Had she attended the same school?

'Were you at the Lancaster school when you were in London?' I asked.

She shook her head.

'No school,' she said. 'Not there.'

I shrugged. It hadn't seemed very likely anyway.

She smiled and then said, 'I have something to show you. Why don't you follow me?'

She must have been exploring the house, I thought, and maybe she had found something that might seem to a child's mind to be of some significance. Bemused, and happy to humour her, I nodded and let her go ahead of me up the stairs and on to the upper floor.

She stopped on the main landing, and I noticed that someone had taken trouble to board up a short expanse of wall, using long wooden planks that had been nailed down across what I guessed might be a doorway. I had no tools with which to make a breach in the wall. If I came back to the house at all, I vowed to tear the planks away and see what lay behind.

I followed her back to the hallway and, as I was about to ask her more about herself, she turned to me and gestured, inviting me to bend down with my ear to her mouth.

'Dominic is with Rose now. With his wife and his ancestors. With your ancestors.'

She smiled and took sudden flight, dashing for the open door. I hurried after her, but when I burst into the open and looked round in both directions, I couldn't see her anywhere. I had found my ghost, or so I reckoned. She hadn't seemed frightening in the least. I still had a lot to understand.

I had decided not to stay in the hotel after all, in fact I could not bear to remain in the Lakes another day. I retrieved my luggage and paid what I owed them, then went down to the landing stage and waited for the next steamer from Glenridding. I boarded the *Lady of the Lake*, the oldest passenger vessel in the world, or so they say, and sat on deck in an attempt to throw off the stifling atmosphere of the old house.

I returned to London later that day. Exhausted and not a little spooked, I said nothing to my wife and children, but went to bed and slept.

Next morning, a thick package was waiting for me on the kitchen table. I recognized the name and address of the family solicitors, Abercrombie, Lund and Humble, who kept offices in Lincoln's Inn.

My wife Jess watched closely as I cut the packet open and reached inside to fish out the contents. These consisted of a letter and several hardback notebooks. I opened the first one. It appeared to consist of handwritten notes, but at the top of the first page someone had written in red ink: 'The Ullswater Diary of Dominic Lancaster RN'. My grandfather. Tucked in between the page and the cover was a medal and a ribbon, Dominic's 1939–1945 Star, awarded him for services at the Battle of Dakar. I put the medal in my pocket. Later that evening, alone in my study, I started reading.

Charles Lancaster
21 March 2012

The Diaries

I used to go to the Lakes as a child. My parents would sweep me up at the start of summer and drive me all the way from London in our Hispano-Suiza H6 and, from the early thirties, the J12. We had a chauffeur, of course, first a man called Higgins, an elderly chap (or so he seemed to me), then Morris, a much younger man. In town, only my mother drove, getting, I think, a measure of pleasure and independence from doing so. And they were very beautiful cars, which added greatly to her enjoyment, for she was something of a snob and an *aficionada* of fine things like Japanese netsuke and, of course, the best Portuguese *azulejo* tilework, which she used in our Oporto home to such great effect. Not that many people had cars back then, and no one of our acquaintance fielded a Hispano-Suiza. For that matter, not many people had a house in the country either, to which they could repair for summer holidays. We went to the Lakes because we Lancasters always went there, apart from our

13

stays in Portugal, which were mainly for business. The Lakes' house was old and went back in the family to the early eighteenth century. Growing up, I felt rather special trundling down country roads almost free of traffic, cocooned in the protected space my mother and father created. I would spend the summer playing with the Howtown children or setting out with my friends Peter and Maurice for trips on the lake, to play pirates or swim out to Cherry Holm Island. I tried to contact them when I arrived here in London last week, only to be told that Peter has already been called up and Maurice has followed in my footsteps and joined the Navy. I wish him better luck afloat than I have known.

I was one of the first casualties of the war. I worked in a non-reserved occupation, in the small advertising department of the family firm. I was twenty-three when hostilities began, and when conscription was brought in that November, I signed up for the Navy in the old church hall where I'd gone once a week as a child to our Cub Scout meetings. There were old friends with me, old Cub Scouts, winking and smiling at each other, walking to our fates. When I was ten years old, I'd hastened to join the local branch of the Sea Cadets, where I learned to climb without flinching the rigging on a tall sailing ship in the heart of a storm. I fancied myself a sailor, and spent more and more of my holidays on Ullswater, sailing on board our little yacht, the *Firefly*, and swimming in the lake's calm waters. The outbreak of war seemed to me such an opportunity, a chance to show I was more than just a businessman being groomed to run the family enterprise, but a real man, perhaps a hero in disguise. My father, who had always thought me a sad disappointment to the family because I loved music more than business and had talked more than once about going to music college, grudgingly accepted my newfound status as a fighting man. He had served in the last war, and I think he believed that this onset of manliness might bring me round to his idea that I should commit to taking over the Lancaster Port House when the time came. At twenty-three, I had never found a girl to walk out with. Some thought me a sissy, others seemed to have their own reasons for turning down my invitations to a dance or the pictures. But now, I thought, a sailor in uniform might catch some glances from the fair sex.

Unfortunately, I wasn't sent to sail on a lake, but on the Norwegian Sea, heading into Vestfjorden bound for Narvik on board the HMS *Hotspur*. The *Hotspur* was an H-class destroyer, and I was a barely-trained gunner stationed at one of her four Mark IX guns. It was when we reached Narvik that things heated up. The Germans had invaded Norway at the start of April, and there was naval fighting outside Narvik on the 8th and 9th. The next day we reached Narvik in the early morning, under cover of a snowstorm. The rest is history, as they say. We sank some German ships, but Jerry returned in force with larger destroyers. The *Hunter* was sent to the bottom by torpedoes, the *Hardy* was badly damaged, and we were hit quite badly, but not enough to finish us off. It might have been better for me if we had been holed below the waterline.

The *Hotspur* was towed off for repairs with a skeleton crew. Along with some others, I was transferred to the HMS *Resolution*, which had also suffered bomb damage. I stayed with her through to June, when we joined Force H at Gibraltar, and then on to Mers-el-Kebir in July. That was my greatest moment. Our fleet destroyed the Vichy French fleet in Algeria, to stop their ships falling into the hands of the Germans. I'm sorry about the French sailors who were killed, for in a way they were our allies; but this was war and we could not afford to go soft when we were fighting a ruthless enemy.

We sailed down the coast of West Africa and reached Dakar

on the 24th September. This time our fleet met more severe opposition than we had anticipated. The day after the main battle, my ship was hit by a torpedo from a French submarine and I felt a shock of pain. I remember nothing of what followed. I must have passed out and stayed unconscious for days.

When I came to my senses I found myself in bed on board a hospital ship. I had a raging thirst and a strange feeling of mugginess. On top of that I was thoroughly confused, having no idea how long had passed since the battle or what had happened to me that had led my hospitalization. Only the rolling of the ship and the sight of white beds on either side of me brought home where I was, on an anonymous ship heading in God knew what direction.

I was just thinking about where I was when a pretty young woman in the uniform of a Queen Alexandra Naval Nurse arrived at my bedside. She smiled at me, and I felt better at once.

'Hello,' she said. 'You've come round, I see.' She had a lovely Scottish accent, and I thought for a moment I'd been taken to one of the Highland Casualty Clearing Stations or a hospital in Inverness or Aberdeen, though I was aware that it was a long way from West Africa to Aberdeen.

'Where am I?' was my first question. Not 'How am I?' or 'How did I get here?' I guessed something must be wrong for me to have been invalided out from the *Resolution*. Had the ship been sunk after all? Was I just one of the survivors, suffering from exposure in Dakar's shark-infested waters?

'You're on board the SS *Aba*,' she said. Her freshly starched uniform and friendly manner reassured me after the shambles at Mers-el-Kebir. 'The *Aba*'s a hospital ship, Lieutenant, the best in the fleet. Lucky we were nearby when your ships got beaten up. You're in safe hands now. But if you'll excuse me, I have to report to Matron that you're back in the land of the living.'

'Before you go,' I said, 'won't you tell me why I'm here? What's wrong with me? Was I hurt in the attack? Apart from being knocked out.'

Her manner changed at once. The banter went out of her voice.

'That's not for me to say, Lieutenant. A doctor will be along soon. He can tell you in a lot more detail.'

With which she trotted off. She hadn't even told me her name. She seemed very young, and it chilled me to think of her in this place, among so many injured, so many dead or dying, so many crying out for help, as I might cry out once I came fully to my senses.

A naval orderly brought me some water to drink and a plate of light food. As I started to eat, I noticed that the man in the bed to my right was in distress. I called for the orderly. He closed the curtain round the bed and went off to fetch help. I felt helpless, not knowing if there was anything I could do. Moments later, three nurses arrived with a doctor in tow. They went behind the curtain and remained there for about half an hour, all the time talking in whispers. When they came out at last, their faces were grave. The nurse who had welcomed me did not even look in my direction. The curtains remained shut. I left my supper untouched: my appetite had gone.

My nurse returned a little later. I knew better than to ask her about what had happened, but I did say I was lost without my watch, a Soway Prima my father had given me before I set off for Norway (though none of us knew where we were headed at the time).

'It's a quarter past ten, dear,' she said. 'We'll be putting the lights out soon. Matron's very strict about the lights. She's on loan from the RAMC, and she's a terribly strict woman. She has no sympathy for nurses, patients and, least of all, doctors.

17

They're all afraid of her, especially the doctors, even the chief surgeon, Sir Ian McKenzie; but they all respect her. They say we should get the War Office to send her to Germany as a secret weapon. Before lights out, you need to have a word with Dr O'Neill. He's Irish, but we've trained him to behave properly to his patients.'

'Do you have a name?' I asked, feeling very bold.

'Nurse MacDonald to you, sir. But if a wee cadet like you has a big brother, he can call me Alice. Now, I'll fetch Dr O'Neill.'

He was close by and came to me in under a minute. I recognized him from the drama earlier. He brought a chair and set it by my bed. I thought he looked tired. Very tired.

'Lieutenant Lancaster. May I sit down?'

I nodded. He seemed to be in his mid-thirties, middle class, well-meaning. I smiled at him in the expectation of some of that prattle well-meaning doctors use. Instead, he was very formal.

'Lieutenant, the good news is that you're alive and generally sound. Your ship was hit by a torpedo from a French submarine called the *Bévézier*, and some of your colleagues were killed. Your gun fell on top of you, but a friend pulled you out and got you into the drink with him. You were in a lifeboat in seconds, which is why you haven't suffered the effects of prolonged immersion in the sea and haven't been eaten by a shark. That's the good news. Tomorrow, you can write to your parents saying you're well and you'll soon be on your way home.'

'If it's that simple, why was I brought here in the first place?'

In a soft Irish burr that I was shortly to hate, he explained.

'If you don't mind, I'll call you Dominic. The thing is, you've been here for three days. Until today, you've been sedated, and you still have a heavy dose of morphia in your veins. I'd like to taper that off, but you'll need some to deal with the pain.'

'But if I'm not badly wounded . . .'

'I didn't say that, Dominic. I'll be quite honest with you. The only way we could save your life when we took you on board was to amputate your left leg below the knee. I'm sorry for your bad luck. It's a very serious thing to happen to a man, a fit young man your age. But the worst is over, and now we must concentrate on getting you back to health and learning what you can do on one leg, which, as it happens, will be much more than you can guess.'

He took leave of me with his good wishes. Moments later, the lights were extinguished. The morphia helped me sleep, but when I woke up the next morning I wanted to scream when I remembered what Dr O'Neill had told me.

Sunday, 17 November

I was explaining how I came to be here, at home, in London. We tied up at the King George V Dock in Glasgow, and most of us were transferred to Mearnskirk Hospital, a sanatorium that had been altered to enable it to take soldiers, sailors and airmen injured in the war. The lucky others, men with light injuries, were sent off home or told to rejoin their regiment or find a new ship. By the time we got to Blighty, heavy air raids were hitting the larger cities, and not just London. I almost wished a bomb might end my misery. I had started to devour myself with grief for my leg, a leg that would no longer let me walk or run or jump.

They started to reduce my dose of morphia, and at times the pain would hit me like a racing car slamming against a careless bystander. The stump was dressed in a huge swaddling of cloths and bandages. Part of me wanted to see the leg itself, to take in the reality I would now be faced with, and part of me

19

wanted nothing to do with it. I feared the pain removing the bandage would cause. Nurse MacDonald had been ordered to stay in order to work with her patients from the *Aba*. Every few days she would inject me with morphia, remove my sheets, set up a screen, and unroll my bandages and packing. She cleaned my wound – or that is what she *said* she did – and bandaged me again. It was uncomfortable. My leg was regaining some feeling. All that kept me together was the knowledge that so many others in the ward where I lived had suffered much greater injuries. Then Alice MacDonald came to see me one day and kissed my forehead and sailed away on another boat. A succession of new nurses took over, none as pretty and none as kind. I regretted her going very much.

I stayed about a fortnight, to the second week in October, and then one of the doctors said I was fit enough to go home, where a district nurse would see to me. I felt suddenly fearful of going back to our house in Bloomsbury, afraid to let my parents and sister see what the war had done to me. I was not, surprisingly, much afraid of the air raids. I had left London amidst such expectations, such promises of medals and fanfares and a job well done, and I would pass again through our front door a miserable failure, someone who would spend his life in a state of dependence on others. I might never find a job, never earn my crust, never find a girl to marry, never have children, never kick a football again, or run on the rugger field. My father's opinion of me would have been proved right after all. It would be crutches or a wheelchair for me from now on. I was twenty-four years old. I had my life ahead of me. Of course, I know our boys had a pounding in France and that this Blitz is killing hundreds, maybe thousands. But if I can't get out and take some revenge on the Germans, then I don't know what is the point of me.

★   ★   ★

My mother and father met me at King's Cross, where I arrived on board a much-delayed troop train. They brought my little sister Octavia with them. The smile on her face when she saw me made up for a lot. She'd been in floods of tears when I last saw her, on the dock as my ship pulled away on the first stage of my journey. They were all in good spirits to see me alive. But I could see Mother glancing again and again at the hump where a cage sat over what was left of my leg, and I sensed that her bonhomie was forced. She would never accept an imperfect man as her son. They had to take me off on a stretcher carried by two porters. There were a lot of wounded on the train, but I was scarcely considered serious. Mother has always been a proud woman, sometimes excessively so, and I knew as well that she'd wanted grandchildren from me, the last of the male line. That was, I knew, unlikely to happen now. Who would marry a one-legged man, half a man?

Octavia held my hand as soon as she could and looked into my eyes, but said nothing of my amputation. She made a slicing motion once at the start, and I nodded. That was all she needed to know. The concern she felt was evident on her face, as her emotions always are. She is an extremely sensitive child, feeling things more acutely than others, especially other people's suffering. I have often found her instinct for pain uncanny. To balance this, she's vivacious, animated and cheerful most of the time, even though she can't communicate most of her emotions through words. Not even my parents have been able to repress her natural instincts for trouble and passion, for her condition inhibits the discipline they would like to impose on her. They do not love her, of course. As I have just written, my mother cannot abide anything with a defect, so Octavia's deafness and my amputated leg are both curses to her. As for my father, he remains as remote from her as custom and duty allow.

21

We drove back to Bloomsbury in the Hispano. I joked that my father must have obtained enough petrol for the trip on the black market, Army petrol as likely as not. Of course, Bloomsbury is next door to King's Cross, so he would only have needed a teaspoonful or two if he'd been in any other car. He sneered at my impertinent sense of humour, as he had done so many times in the past. I said nothing in reply; I was glad enough to do the journey in private transport.

We made good time: there was very little traffic on the road. The bombs were scaring people away, but Father was confident that Bloomsbury wouldn't be hit as hard as the East End, or perhaps not at all. 'There's nothing of strategic importance here,' he said. Octavia could do nothing to cheer me up: in the front passenger seat, I couldn't see her hands move or her lips make words, but she did what she could in speech. I think I'm the only person who understands some of what she says. My parents couldn't care less and leave her in the keeping of a succession of tutors who try to remedy her 'defect' with little science and no art at all.

We got back to Bloomsbury in time for the blackout. This was only brought in about a month ago, and I'd been put asleep early in the hospital, so it was completely new to me and very disconcerting. With the winter coming in, the heavy curtains hemmed us about and gave a sense of darkness to everything. Father had installed a shelter in the living room, pinning corrugated sheets to the ceiling and reinforcing it all with stout wooden posts. He said these indoor shelters were a better option than the Andersons that let in water and were cold and damp. The square management committee had debated whether they should put an Anderson in the garden at the centre of the square, but someone had suggested that we'd be invaded by the occupants of all the flats around us, so the residents had opted for the indoor style instead.

That evening my parents spoke to the consultant whom they paid to take over my case. He was a grey-faced man from the south of England, Mr Longmate. He wore little pince-nez spectacles, from which he looked down at me as a diner might look on a dish of braised kidneys. I suspected he was telling them things he would not impart to me. He was a cold fish, not given to encouraging comments. His premises are in Harley Street, of course. I was glad to see the back of him when he left. He had hardly spoken to me, only to my parents, and mostly to my mother.

My father spent most of the evening in his office. He is a wine shipper specializing in *vinho do porto* from Portugal. Our family has owned a *quinta* at São João da Pesqueira since 1730. I have been there twice, but I fear I will never return, for the steep slopes would defeat me. We grow some grapes ourselves, mainly the Tinta Barroca and Tinta Cão varieties. Father runs one of the country's most successful import firms and has close ties to Portugal's fascist prime minister, Mr Salazar. We have a large office in Porto, where our label is respected along with those of Taylor, Croft, and Warre's. As a result, he is in much demand to speak at Rotary Club branches or the Chamber of Commerce. He's not given to displays of emotion, and I believe he does not feel any, but I can see he is under pressure. German U-boats are threatening shipping in the Atlantic, and getting shipments from Oporto must be hard and dangerous.

18 November

Today Dr Longman visited again, and again spoke chiefly to my mother. I have slept for the most part, and Octavia has sat by my side. Our housekeeper, Mrs Mayberry, brings food to tempt me, and I eat a little only for Octavia's sake. Being half a man, there seems not much point in anything now.

I stayed at home throughout the rest of November, but I quickly sensed that, apart from my father's business worries and the anxiety that focused on my leg and my uncertain future, something else was troubling both my parents. The retreat from Dunkirk in May had proved destabilizing for both of them, and they often talked about what it might foreshadow. If we couldn't stop the Germans in France, what chance would we have of beating them with our backs to the wall here? Would Hitler invade Spain and Portugal or use Franco and Salazar as his go-betweens? In a way, I was glad my father spoke of such possibilities, because I considered it defeatist talk and told him so. My war was over, but I couldn't bear to hear someone give encouragement to the enemy. He cooled down after that and retreated back inside his shell.

Octavia was barely affected by any of this. I didn't tell her much. She knew about the war, for she could hardly fail to have noticed the air-raid shelters, the barrage balloons, the men and women in uniform on the streets. But her deafness meant that she never heard the air-raid sirens howl or the all-clear sound. She's an affectionate child, though she received little of affection from her mother and father. She doesn't have friends, apart from children she knows from the deaf school she occasionally visits. Other little girls – there are or were several in the square – avoid her, since they have no way of communicating with her, thinking her stupid, something she most certainly is not. At least Mrs Mayberry is kind to her, and Octavia spends so much of her time in the kitchen. And it has taken my mind off my own sufferings to devote time to improving Octavia's reading

24

and writing. She has skills well beyond her age, since most of her focus has been on the written language and, as I said, she is far from stupid.

There is one thing for which she is never appreciated: her laugh. It is an unrestrained laugh – more a cackle, really – that creases her face and sometimes bends her double. It grates on most people, for it bears little resemblance to what they consider a proper laugh. I have always liked it, because I have always understood Octavia. When she laughs, her whole being is in it, her eyes shine, tears run down her cheeks. It is the most natural and unaffected laugh you can hope to hear. When she was younger, I used to tickle her, and that would send her into paroxysms of mirth. She stands out in a house so full of meaningful silences. Here, when anyone pretends to laugh, all that comes out is a stilted, well-controlled snigger. They have always tried to stop her laughing, but from my late teens I've made an effort to keep her doing so. I know how to make the sort of jokes she likes. I make funny faces, I jump around like a mad thing. Well, perhaps not now, but I did.

I asked my mother not to admit any neighbours, for some people we know have heard of my misfortune and several have expressed a desire to visit. No doubt they mean well, but I'm not in the mood for tea and cakes with a dollop of pity on the side. My mother says that, if they do call, all they will talk about is the war. But I tell her that the war is precisely the topic that will encourage people to talk about my leg and its absence.

Father came in last week. He was heading for his office, but said there was something he wanted to talk to me about. I was sitting up in bed now. The district nurse, a middle-aged woman called Mrs Bainbridge, had come in to dress my leg and, being a rather bossy sort of woman, had insisted I learn how to sit up, which I now did, bracing myself on my complete leg.

'Dominic,' Father said, 'I have a concern I'd like to share with you.'

It wasn't like him to share things with anyone, most of all his own family. We Lancasters were too long in the tooth, too bound by tradition, too little cosseted by sympathy, and what Lancasters had done two hundred years ago, Lancasters were expected to do today. According to my mother, my father has for some years been in eager anticipation of a knighthood – I really cannot say for what – and was growing uneasy about it, for he thought it likely that the new king would confer honours only on those who had contributed to the war work. I suspect he has been working behind the scenes to contrive some sort of deal with Salazar for the export of wolfram, which is an essential metal to harden machine edges for the manufacture of armaments. Portugal has almost as much wolfram as China, and Salazar sells unlimited quantities to the Third Reich. I think Father uses his good offices through contacts in Lisbon, which seems to be the spy capital of the world. He knows the ins and outs of the Portuguese bureaucracy.

Yet, Father sat down on the edge of the bed and tried to smile. I waited for whatever was to come.

'Son, I don't have to tell you about the air raids. They're going up and down the country now. Liverpool's been hit, Manchester, Birmingham, London, and it's spreading every night. They say it will get a lot worse before it stops, when Goering runs out of planes, if he ever does. London's been hit much more heavily than most. You know Octavia wasn't able to join the big evacuation last September because her condition means she needs extra help. But evacuation is a lot more urgent than it was two Septembers ago. Octavia can't go just anywhere. Your mother and I have to stay in London – I have to take care of the office, and she insists on lending a hand with the WVS here in

Bloomsbury. We'll stick it out, but Octavia's another matter. She can't hear the alerts or the all-clears, she can't hear much of the bombs, and she's headstrong. We've caught her more than once heading outside after blackout, set to wander off Heaven knows where.

'You're not happy here, we can see that. So I want you to take Octavia up to the Lakes, to Ullswater, and open up Hallinhag House. What do you say?'

I looked at him askance. There had been so many changes for me since Dakar, my head was spinning with places and people.

'Father, wouldn't I be more use to you by staying in London and starting work in the office? I've worked there before, and I'm sure I can pick up the rest once . . .'

He put up his hand and shook his head.

'Dominic, you're in no fit state to start working in the office again at a time like this. You've never shown any serious interest before. Perhaps when the war is over you can be trusted to do some simple tasks. But I don't care to have you in the business right now.'

'You've been planning this ever since you knew I was coming home,' I said. 'How do you expect me to cope over at the lake when I can't handle things here?'

He nodded. I wondered why he hadn't asked my mother to take part in the charade.

'Octavia will look after you,' he said. 'She's had to be a capable child, and you're the only one who can communicate with her. There's a district nurse from Pooley Bridge who'll visit you most days and look after your medical needs.'

I didn't have much choice. How could I rebel? I couldn't leave without help, and however much my leg troubled me, I knew I'd get little sympathy in a world where people were dying violently in large numbers every day. Don't get me wrong, I do love my little sister dearly, but out here she's my only company.

We were driven up by Morris, a taciturn man, chosen because my father did not want to chat to his driver to and from work.

Hallinhag House has belonged to the family for over two hundred years, with bouts of refurbishment on the ground floor and the roof thrown in every few decades, and we all know it well. Except Octavia, who has never been here owing to her asthma. Of course, that has improved a lot over the past few years, and my parents consulted with Dr Hammell, who declared her fit to stay in a lakeside house. And if she does have an attack, it won't be hard to get her home again. Actually, it will, won't it? If there's no one else here, I can't take her to Howtown, I can't drive, and there's no telephone out here.

She has just stepped into the living room, where I have my bed and bits and pieces. She's wearing her summer clothes: the pink cardie I gave her last year for her birthday, the blue skirt Mother bought to go with it, and those bright red shoes she simply won't take off. She will need to put on something more, because it's already very cold.

She looks at me and grins. She has tied her black hair back in a chignon, something my mother taught her to do. It makes her look very grown up.

'Your nurse will be here tomorrow,' she says.

I moan. I don't want a nurse.

'She'll be fat and bossy,' I tell her, using lips and hands to make words.

She grins again, then gestures, 'It's chilly in here, don't you think?'

'A little,' I reply, though I know perfectly well it's cold enough to freeze the sheep to death on their lonely hills. But I'm wrapped up warmly in bed, and my senses are still dimmed by morphia. I fear a life like this, immobile, dependent on the warm hearts of friends and my sister and the cold hands of nurses and doctors when they choose to come. I dream of Alice Mac-Donald, my gentle nurse, and summon her in my sleep. She has tended thousands like me.

'I left Boris behind,' Octavia gestured.

'How awful,' I said. Boris was the teddy bear she had had since the age of one or so. A furry beast with a red button for one eye. She had sewn the button there herself, about a year ago. Just the one eye, disabling him, bringing him closer to her.

The house seems more than quiet. Downcast. Full of memories. No, that's wrong. It's full of forgettings. All the years that have gone, and I know so little of the men and women who spent time here, even though they were my ancestors. When I have been here before, the house has seemed filled with light; but that was always the summer, and it is winter now. Perhaps the house has picked up my mood, sensed my new vulnerability, and knows how useless I am. Can houses sense what we feel? Do they feed off all the emotions that have been experienced between their walls? Octavia says there are ghosts here. I admonish her, and I watch her when she comes to this room. She might be serious, but I doubt it. She has no names for these ghosts. Maybe they are silent, like her.

Monday, 9 December

My new nurse called this morning. She tells me she will be my permanent carer, subject to war conditions, which means she'll attend me one day at a time. Her name is Rose Sansom, and she's both a Queen's Nurse and a district nurse. She's based in

Pooley Bridge on the northern tip of Ullswater, but she reports each month to Barrow-in-Furness, where the Cumbrian HQ of the Queen's Nurses is based.

I was wrong. Rose isn't fat and she's no bossier than any nurse I've dealt with till now. In fact, she's very slim and as pretty as her name, and I feel quite smitten. I'll have to watch myself. Of course, she has the upper hand. She cleaned and dressed my wound with the greatest gentleness, just as Alice MacDonald used to do. It hurt, as it always does, but I put on a brave face throughout, and I fancy it hurt less than before. She's the first nurse since Alice I've had confidence in.

'You're healing well,' she said as she finished putting on a new bandage and fastening it with adhesive tape.

'You nurses all say that,' I objected. 'You don't have to keep the truth from me.'

She gave me a look I shall never forget. She's quite short, with short auburn hair and soft red lips. I've already learned that she can look at me in a hundred different ways, all of them capable of making me uncomfortable.

'I never mollycoddle my patients,' she retorted. 'Whatever I tell you will be the truth, however unpalatable it may be. We'll get on well if you learn to trust me.'

I nodded timidly, well admonished. Of course, I didn't tell her I trusted her already. It's not the done thing. Or is that just my family's attitude, where nobody ever trusts anybody, except Octavia and myself? She made me feel something of a child, though from the look of her I guess she's a year or two younger than myself.

As she was helping me back into my pyjamas, the door opened and I saw Octavia come in. They had met earlier, when Nurse Sansom arrived, but now I introduced them properly. Nurse Sansom wasn't in the least flustered by Octavia's disability as so many are. She made sure she was looking straight at her when she spoke, and she was able to do some primitive gesturing, which delighted Octavia no end.

When Octavia left again, Rose – for that is what she already insisted I call her – sat beside me again.

'Tell me about Octavia,' she said.

I told her what there was to know. That she'd been born with good hearing but that at the age of five she'd contracted mumps and gone completely deaf. Rose listened gravely, and I had a feeling that she took a special interest in the matter.

'I'd like to help her,' she said. 'I have a cousin, John, aged fifteen, who was deaf from birth. He's been to all manner of teachers and advisers, most of them useless. But a couple of years ago he was fitted with a hearing aid. Doesn't Octavia have one?'

I shook my head.

'We heard they weren't very good.'

'Well, that's understandable, the new type were only developed a few years back. But they can do a lot of good. I'll look into what's possible. I take it your family have money?'

It was hard to dissemble. The house itself and its furnishings spoke for themselves, and though I was bed-bound, I was wearing a smoking jacket that had been bought in Paris at a little shop my mother knew, in an impasse in St Germain.

'Normally, quite a lot. With the war, things aren't so good.'

'Well, if she gets an Amplivox, it shouldn't cost more than thirty pounds. It's a lot of money, but if your parents can meet the cost . . .'

Just then, Octavia came in again, gesturing.

'I've been in the kitchen,' she said. 'It's really cold. It's even cold in here.'

The living room, which I had made my bedroom and general quarters, was piping hot. A large wood fire was blazing in the fireplace, and Rose had told me that the weather outside was mild. The room is Octavia's bedroom as well, where she sleeps on a French sleigh bed that my mother had ordered down from one of the rooms upstairs.

Rose called Octavia to her and used a thermometer to take her temperature.

'Normal,' she said. 'But if you still feel cold, Octavia, I'll take you up to Pooley Bridge to see Dr Raverat.'

She said goodbye after that and said she'd pop in again tomorrow. Octavia saw her to the door.

Wednesday, 11 December

This is, God knows, as lonely a place as I have known. I have Octavia for company, of course, but she is ten years old, and I often want to speak with an adult, a man or even a woman. Of course, with a woman I can never expect any more than intelligent conversation. All I can hope for is to have some women for my friends. The loss of my leg has diminished me so completely, I scarcely think of myself as a man now, a proper man, well formed, active, not the partial thing I have become.

The sense of isolation here is made worse in the long evenings and nights. The blackout hems us in, but I had forgotten that the house was never fitted with either gas or electricity, and that we must depend on candles and oil lamps of various kinds. When dark comes down, the house changes. It is all shadows, shadows that shift and change. I feel disturbed by it. Lying alone in my bed, I am trapped, and my mind fixes on the shadows and the way the flickering of a candle will send them scurrying in all directions. Sometimes they will cluster in a corner, and my imagination fancies that they move of their own accord, or that someone is watching me from within them. I keep a lamp burning through the night. Octavia sleeps on the sleigh bed at the foot of mine and says she does not mind the shaded light. At times she whimpers in her sleep, but I do not think she can hear the small sounds the house makes as its wooden beams expand and contract.

Rose came again today. She arrived by car instead of bicycle. It's Dr Raverat's car, a little TB Midget, bright red and striking, even with its folding roof securely in place. I realized that the doctor must trust her a lot, to let her drive on these country roads in such a smart little sports car.

She had a reason for borrowing it.

'I prefer my bicycle,' she said, 'but I've brought something that wouldn't fit safely on a bike.'

She went out to the car, and when she came back in she was carrying a pair of wooden crutches.

I recoiled when I saw them. 'Oh no,' I said. 'I'm not ready for those.' I was terrified at the thought of them, of going outside, of falling on my back, of crashing on to my face, catching them in weeds, displaying my awkwardness, like a child learning to walk for the first time. Frankly, I didn't want them at all.

She smiled and approached the bed.

'The sooner you can get out of that bed and start to walk, the better you'll feel. You're stifling in here and getting bedsores.'

'I don't have any clothes.'

She laughed.

'Octavia has shown me where your things are kept.'

As if on cue, Octavia arrived, carrying a pair of trousers, a sock, a shirt and a thick pullover that I had worn against the cold of the fjords. She grinned and laid the bundle on top of her bed, then made her way back to the kitchen, where she lived while she was not with me.

'Shouldn't I do this in hospital?'

Rose shook her head.

'Lieutenant, what can I do to make you understand? I am a trained nurse. I have won awards for my nursing. I have worked in two hospitals, and I have seen my fill of amputated legs. Or, in your case, a partially amputated leg. You are already luckier than many men I have looked after: you have a complete leg and half a leg. There are men whose legs begin and end at the top of their thighs. I have dressed wounds, as I intend to dress yours today. Your wound is healing up nicely, but I want you out of bed. As it is, you've been bedridden too long. Dr Raverat agrees. He says you've been too long on your back. I don't like to criticize anyone, but I've already seen that soldiers and sailors don't always get the best medical attention. The longer you stay in bed, the more likely it is that liquid will go to your lungs and cause pneumonia. In your weakened state, that could be very dangerous indeed.'

She stayed for the rest of the day, getting me dressed, holding me while I made my way up on to the crutches, lifting me, touching me with infinite care. I felt myself slipping further and further towards her. She walked me round the living room in circles. Without her I would have tripped, and any time she relaxed her hold, I felt myself tilt and head for a fall. But her hands were always ready to catch me. Although I had no prosthetic limb, I slowly learned to balance on the crutches without one. An artificial leg, she said, would come later, perhaps in a week or two, but she wanted Dr Raverat to examine me before I even attempted to walk on one.

She got me back to bed an hour before nightfall, which came just after five.

'I want to get this car back to Dr Raverat,' she said. 'I don't fancy driving without headlights on these roads. I'd probably drive straight into the lake.'

'You're welcome to stay here,' I said. 'We have enough for dinner.'

She shook her head.

'Thanks, but I have no choice. The doctor is going out on his rounds tonight. He likes to see his patients when they're at home.'

I frowned.

'Surely they'd be in bed?'

'Not all of them. Only the really sick ones. Most of them head out to work as soon as they've been given their medicine. They're in reserved occupations and they don't want anybody to start thinking they aren't really necessary and sending them into the Army.'

'Or the Navy.'

She laughed. It was a lovely laugh, like water running over the stones in a brook.

I wondered what it would be like to have a woman like that for my own, but my eyes fell on the crutches, which had been left near to hand.

She said goodbye and Octavia came in. I hadn't let her watch me on the crutches.

'Don't you think a wheelchair would be better?' I asked her.

She shook her head.

'I asked Rose about that. She says it would only be an option if you had lost all of your leg. She wants you to try the crutches and not give in. I think she likes you.'

Although all this was said in silence, her last words struck me as if she'd shouted in my ear.

She came to the bedside.

'Dominic, can I tell you something?'

'Of course. You know you can tell me anything, dear.'

She seemed thoughtful, possibly anxious. I couldn't imagine what might have happened. Octavia has always been mature for her age, forced as she is to spend less time with other children than she might have liked. She said nothing at first, whether verbally or in gestures. Then she spoke without sound, using her lips to express with some care what she wanted to say. And she took out the paper tablet on which she could write in pencil and began to scribble.

'When you were with Rose,' she wrote, 'I went out to buy some food for supper. I brought the ration book with me. There's only one shop in Howtown, so I marched in and smiled at the lady behind the counter. She let me register for us both, even though I'm really young, but when she looked over what I'd written, including our address, she looked at me, as though I frightened her. Well, I know about funny looks from people, and maybe she's never seen a deaf person before, but I thought it odd. She fetched everything I wanted and stamped the book, but even as I was leaving she kept her eyes on me.'

'Well, I think you're right, love. She may not have seen anyone like you in Howtown before. It's a tiny hamlet. Was she a young woman or older?'

'Much older. An old lady, I'd say.'

'Well, she must surely have set eyes on a deaf person before. No doubt she was puzzled more by your being a foreigner, someone from out of town. All these places are very parochial, you know.'

'That wasn't all,' Octavia continued. 'As I was coming back here, I looked up and I saw a face looking out of the front bedroom window. I couldn't see it very well, and then it disappeared. It might have been the light. I thought it was Rose, but she was down here with you when I got in.'

36

'Have you gone upstairs to look?' I asked.

She shook her head.

'I don't like to,' she said. 'What if there was really someone there?'

'Well, I'm no help to you. I think the light got you imagining things. I'm sure no one has broken in. Are you sure there was a face?'

'Not sure,' she wrote. 'It seemed like that.'

'Then just ignore it. It was a trick of the light.'

She smiled wanly, but I do not think she was convinced.

Octavia ventured into the kitchen to prepare supper, which was to be Spam fritters with potatoes – Mrs Mayberry had taught her some basic cooking skills, and she was better than many adults. I began to wish I could use my crutches so I could help her in the kitchen and sit down at the dining-room table. I thought it might be a good idea to find a local woman to come in a couple of times a day in order to make our meals. The smell of the fritters frying wafted in strongly, then I noticed it change. Very quickly, I noticed it become more of a burned smell, mixed with something unpleasant that I couldn't place. There was no point in my shouting, she wouldn't have heard me. I just lay back, hoping she hadn't burned anything. If the kitchen was on fire the house could burn down. Hallinhag House is built solidly from stone, but it is lined with oak beams that may have come from the woods all about us; once a fire caught I was sure the whole structure would catch flame and incinerate anyone inside, especially someone with one leg.

I pulled back the bedclothes and swung myself into a sitting position, dragging my stump as I did so and crying out with the pain. As I did so, the door to the room opened wide and I saw Octavia standing with a tray in her hands. She came in, pushing the door shut behind her with her heel, and headed for the little table we'd brought into the room for meals. There she put the tray down. A delicious smell rose from the food.

'Are you getting up after all?' she asked, without even looking at me.

'Octavia, did you smell the terrible smell just now?'

She turned and gestured, frowning.

'You mean this? I can throw it away if you don't like it. But there's not much in the larder.'

'No, I meant the burning smell. It must have been out with you in the kitchen, or at least that's what I thought.'

She shook her head and looked at me as if I wasn't all there. Like many deaf people, she had a well-developed sense of smell and certainly would have noticed anything as strong as the odour I'd just detected. Perhaps it had been something in the room, I thought, and had gone as suddenly as it had come. I could no longer smell it. Or it may have come from outside, maybe someone was burning something in the woods. I stopped guessing and we ate in silence. I switched on the little radio I'd brought down with me. Radio Eireann was playing 'The Phantom Melody' by Ketèlbey. It was at such times I most pitied Octavia, for there was none of this lovely music she could hear. She had to pass her life in almost total silence.

We had just finished our meal when there was a knock at the door. Octavia went out and came back accompanied again by Rose.

'I hope I'm not interrupting anything,' she said. 'But I was a little concerned about you, so I thought I'd cycle back to pop my head round the door and see how you are. Also, I have good news. Tom Wilkinson in Keswick called to say he has made a nice prosthetic leg for you. I telephoned him two days ago and he told me he'd set to work on it right away. Nothing's too good for a war hero, he tells me. You'll like the leg. He makes them out of wood and leather, and they fit well. All the pressure's on the leg and the knee, no need to press on the pad. He'll bring it over tomorrow and I'll bring it here and fit it.'

I asked her if she'd eaten. She shook her head.

'I was looking forward to some sardines back home. But if you're offering, whatever you have will do me fine. It feels like I haven't eaten since last year.'

'Where is home?' I asked. Octavia ran off to cook some sausages, one of the few things that weren't rationed.

'I'm from round here originally,' she said. 'I had my first job in Keswick after training at the cottage hospital there, that's how I know Tom. Then I was moved back to Pooley Bridge when old Ethel Scanlan headed off overseas with the Queen Alexandria crowd. My dad died seven years ago, and I still live with my mum.'

Her sausages arrived along with some potatoes I'd left over. She devoured them, and I could see she'd been hungry.

'Is it just you and your mum?' I asked, thinking I might be skating on thin ice and adding, 'or are you with your husband?'

She almost choked.

'Husband? What husband? Have you not noticed I have no rings on my fingers?'

'I thought that might be for nursing reasons.'

Sausages downed, she gave me a quick examination to check I hadn't overdone things. She ran her fingers along my left thigh, and used a stethoscope to check the blood supply.

'Don't forget,' she said, letting her hand lie gently on my leg, 'that if there's ever anything you need, whatever it is, you've only to ask.'

She looked at me intently, and it dawned on me that perhaps she didn't mean helping me with a crutch.

'By the way,' she said, 'something funny happened to me as I was coming back here on my bike. As I rode along the track between Howtown and here, I noticed a light in one of your upstairs windows. I thought at first you might have made your way upstairs on the crutches, but a moment's thought told me that was highly unlikely. It must have been Octavia, but I didn't think she liked to go upstairs in the dark, even with a lamp.'

'That's right.'

I told her what Octavia had told me earlier. When she looked at Octavia, my sister just looked back at her and nodded.

'I'll go up,' she said.

'I can't let you do that. If you hold me, I can make it to the top.'

She shook her head.

'Not for one moment. If you fell, you might fall backwards and break your neck at the bottom. Someone may have broken in, some kids perhaps. Just let me take a look.'

She saw my number 8 torch on my bedside table and picked it up with a look of triumph on her face.

'I have one of these,' she said, 'but I can never find a number 8 battery for love or money. If you know where you can find some, just let me know.'

Before I could expostulate further, she tripped out of the room. I heard her climb the stairs, then waited in silence. I could hear her footsteps as she moved from room to room. It took around five minutes, then the door opened and she stepped back in.

'Octavia,' she said, 'be a good girl and make some tea for us. Milk and sugar if you have them.'

Octavia sighed and got to her feet. She liked doing things for Rose, but it was near her bedtime. When she had gone, Rose sat down beside me.

'No burglars,' she said. 'But then I didn't think there were any. Dominic, has Octavia been upstairs?'

I shook my head.

'Not that I know of. I really don't think so.'

'Has she told you why she's reluctant to go up there?'

'Just that she doesn't like the atmosphere.'

'Hmm. You see, that's the problem. I don't like the atmosphere up there either. I've always been a sensible woman. I've studied nursing, which is very scientific. I don't believe in witches or ghosts. But upstairs just now, I felt something that I couldn't see or touch or hear, and I don't know what to make of it.'

'Are you saying the house is haunted?'

I'm a sceptic too, and any talk of the supernatural annoys me. Of course, I had no wish to get annoyed with Rose. She's the best thing in my life at the moment, and I don't want to get some battleaxe in exchange and chase her away.

'I don't know what to say, Dominic. But I don't think you and your sister should go up those stairs until we know what it really is.'

Octavia returned with the teas and some biscuits that had been baked by Rose's mother. Baking is hard during rationing, as we all know, but I was very impressed by what Mrs Sansom had produced. We sat eating our biscuits and drinking tea – complete with milk and sugar – but neither Rose nor I could muster up any conversation at first, and sat with our own thoughts, unwilling to share them for fear of generating a crisis.

I thought Rose might leave, but there was still tea in the pot. Pouring it out I asked about her mother, what sort of woman she was.

'She's getting older now, but she's still the cook in a restaurant for tourists. There's plenty of work for her in spring and summer, but less for the rest of the year. In winter, she sews

41

nick-nacks for the tourist shops for them to sell come summer. Teddy bears and such: she's very good. She'll knit you a hat, if you like.'

I smiled.

'Octavia might like a teddy bear. She left Boris behind in London. I'll have to pay, of course.'

Her face lit up.

'My mum's teddy bears are the best in England. Wait and see. You'll get a discount as my patient.'

I shook my head vigorously.

'No discount, or I'll cancel the order. Anyway, I'm quite a rich patient, so tell her she can overcharge.'

'It's a deal,' she said.

'How did your father die?' I asked. 'He can't have been very old.'

'He was the captain of the *Lady of the Lake*. One of his passengers fell overboard, a little boy. My father jumped in to save him, but a current caught him and pulled him under.'

'And the boy?'

'Someone else managed to hook him back on board. They took him to the infirmary, but he survived. He was a rich boy like you were, a scholar at Eton.'

'Did his parents do anything to compensate for your father's loss?'

She sighed and shook her head. 'They went back to Manchester without a further word. My mother went out to cook and sew.'

I shook my head in disgust.

'Some rich people don't deserve what they have.'

She reached across the table and put her hand briefly on top of mine.

'Would you have compensated my family, Dominic?'

I laughed.

'If it were up to me, the answer is "yes". But if it were down to my father or mother, they'd probably demand that you pay them. They'd probably say it was all your father's fault for sailing badly.'

'You don't seem too happy with your father. Or is that just something you say when you're talking to commoners like myself?'

'If you ever meet my father, you'll take that back. I admired him as a child, but once I got old enough to see what was going on, I learned to stay out of his way.'

'What you need, Dominic Lancaster, is a woman. Someone who'll stick with you through thick and thin, who'd take an interest in you.'

I sniffed.

'I'm not much to be interested in. There's a lot less of me now than there was a couple of months ago.'

'Sometimes with amputees,' she picked up on my jest, 'they find there's more of them afterwards than before. It will change your attitude to everything. It's too early for you yet, but give it time. If we were to meet again a year from now, I'd find you a different person. But you were going to tell me about your family.'

I explained about the Lancasters' long-standing involvement with Portugal and the port trade. She hung on my every word, fascinated by this exotic business of which she'd had no notion until then. She had never taken a glass of port, so I told her where she could find a bottle and some glasses with a decanter. I decanted the wine and poured two glasses. We sipped at them as we talked. She said she liked it. The irises of her eyes were a dark amber colour, and the candles caught fire in them.

'Of course,' I said, 'things have grown difficult for us since the

43

war started. Portugal's a neutral country, but the English have had a treaty with it since 1373. That was the Anglo-Portuguese Treaty, and it was ratified in 1386 with the Treaty of Windsor. It's the oldest alliance in the world. So Portugal still sends goods to us. They have the largest deposits of wolfram in Europe, and they use it to keep both sides happy. They ship some white wine and some port, as well as wine from Madeira, but it's hard to get ships and ensuring deliveries if you do get them. Our last shipment was sent to the bottom of the Atlantic by a U-boat.

'We do have a large warehouse outside London, where we keep some barrels under strict conditions. And we provide some very fine ports to Buckingham Palace and the House of Lords, where there is always a demand. Ten-year-old crusted ports, some forty-year-old vintages, with some cheaper bottles for the wider market. But our stocks are running low, and we aren't replenishing them as quickly as my father would like.'

She decided that she definitely liked the port and was enthralled by what I told her about Portugal. I had only been there a few times, but on one holiday I had taken up the Portuguese guitar, a very different creature to the standard Spanish instrument. I once dreamed of taking it up professionally and playing for *fado* singers in Lisbon.

'I'll get my parents to send one up from London,' I said. 'I should practise anyway, and the present moment is the perfect excuse.'

I was greatly tempted to ask her to stay the night, but thought she might misunderstand my motives, or, understanding them, find them cause for scorn. She left on her bicycle and Octavia locked the door.

I've been sleeping badly tonight, no doubt because of what Rose and Octavia had told me about the upstairs. My dreams were dark, for I saw shapes moving in semi-darkness, shapes that were neither human nor something else, shapes with veils across their eyes, dressed in black or grey, swaying, watching me from a short distance and always coming closer and mumbling what seemed to be words but were not words of any earthly kind, shapes with long, slim hands and fingers that separated light from darkness. In the dreams I saw children with white faces, but not children of this earth, not dead and not alive, not physical children yet warm, their eyes like dead eyes, yet awake. Somewhere words were repeated, but I could not quite make them out, and as I wake in these early hours, the cries are echoing through my mind and have not yet quite left.

Thursday, 12 December

When Octavia and I woke, it was still early and freezing cold. Rose told me yesterday that the forecasters said we'd have Arctic weather this winter, after last year's mild conditions. It certainly felt Arctic first thing. I was reminded of Narvik and the days I had spent freezing on those waters.

There were no disturbances of any kind during the morning, as far as I could tell. After lunch, Rose returned, bringing with her a man she introduced as Dr Raverat. He is a gentleman in his forties, tall and slender of build, mild of disposition, and quick to act. Rose had told him that we thought someone had broken in, and had been seen upstairs yesterday afternoon and later. She said nothing of the unpleasant sensations she and Octavia had experienced.

Together, they went upstairs, alert for anything suspicious that might still be there, but when they came back down they admitted that they had seen nothing. The doctor said he had noticed a smell in the main bedroom, of burning or something very like it, but though he had searched diligently, he had found no trace of a fire in the room itself or in the large fireplace or, so far as he could tell, higher up in the chimney. It had been a false alarm, he said. He did find a dead raven covered in soot in the hearth, which he disposed of in the compost heap at the back of the house. It, he thought, may have been responsible for our disturbance, and it may well have dislodged enough ancient soot, and who could tell what else, giving rise to the burned smell.

The doctor examined me, paying special attention to my leg.

'Well, young man,' he said as he asked Rose to re-dress my stump, 'I'd say you've got off quite lightly, though it may not seem that way to you now. A lot of the war wounded I see in Carlisle are in a bad way, and likely to go on much like that. Last week I saw a man younger than yourself, a boy really, who'd lost both arms. Nurse Sansom here will get you up and about, have no doubt of it. You won't know yourself by Christmas. You won't have me to thank for it either. The first person to bring you round will be yourself. We medical people can't do anything without your help. The second most important person is Nurse Sansom. You may not know it, but she's one of the best nurses I've ever worked with. She'll take good care of you and she'll keep you going every time you may feel like giving up. Just so long as you don't go round falling in love with her, you'll have nothing to worry about.'

I blushed, for I am indeed falling in love with her already. I think she noticed, but she looked away and continued to fasten my leg with her customary skill. I thought she would leave with the doctor, but he stood and made his apologies, saying he had some urgent appointments back in Pooley Bridge. At the door he turned.

'You've missed the daffodils,' he said. 'Just across the lake from here, about four miles away, on Gowbarrow Fell. It's a desperately romantic spot. I'm sure Nurse Sansom will take you there in the spring. They are the very descendants of the ones Dorothy and William Wordsworth saw during a walk here in 1802. He wrote the poem not long afterwards.'

'I've never heard of them,' I said. 'I know the poem, but that's all.' My parents weren't really literary types, and though I'd read the poem at school, I'd never realized the real daffodils were so near to hand.

'They're a glorious sight. But, as I said, you'll have to wait till spring.'

'I may not be here by spring,' I replied. Rose looked at me askance, as though my still being in Hallinhag by the end of winter was a certain thing.

The doctor left. They'd brought her bicycle in the back of the vehicle, for Rose to get back on. They had also brought my artificial leg. She brought it in, carrying it in one hand to show how light it was. My spirits sank as I understood that this would be a key part of my life from here on.

My trousers were still on the bed. Rose came to me, a little brisk at first, then growing more solicitous as things progressed.

'We're going outside,' she said. 'You're going to take me for a walk. Although there's no need to look for daffodils today.'

'But it's freezing outside,' I protested. 'You said so yourself. I haven't been outside for weeks, and now it's winter. When I was last outside for any time, I was off the African coast.'

'For goodness' sake,' she exclaimed, 'act like a man. You're not a baby, and your body can take anything the winter throws at you in its stride. Staying indoors, staying in bed isn't doing you any good, alongside the morphia.'

47

'What if I fall?' I felt crushed by the sudden change in her attitude.

'Then you'll pick yourself up and keep walking. Listen to me, Dominic, I'm sorry if I sound harsh, but if I let you off the hook you'll wind up bedridden, and that's the last thing any of us need. If we're to be friends, you have to pull yourself together and make me proud of you. I can only admire a man who acts like a man. You did well to join the Navy and go into battle twice, but this is your real battle and you have to do most of it yourself.'

She helped me dress, let me lean on her while I stood, and held me while I took hold of the crutches and fixed them beneath my arms. I was stung by what she said, but I could hardly deny the truth of it.

We asked Octavia to stay behind. Rose thought her asthma might be activated by the cold.

'I know someone who makes herbal remedies,' said Rose. 'I'm not supposed to encourage such things, but I know very well that this woman's treatments work in some cases. I'll ask her to call in some day.'

Outside, the light was good. My movements were uncertain. I had to balance on each crutch in turn while I moved the other forward. Of course, this was easy enough when I could lean on my good leg, but I was still awkward with the amputation. But even there I found the artificial leg would bear my weight better than I at first imagined. And Rose clung to me by my left arm, very like a sweetheart, though I dared not let my thoughts stray in that direction.

We walked down to the lake shore. As we did so we noticed four children standing a little further up, watching us, a boy of about sixteen and three girls of about ten or eleven.

'Do you know them?' I asked.

Rose shook her head.

'I've never seen them before. They do look an odd bunch, though. I imagine the youngest girl is about ten and the oldest twelve. The boy is a few years older. They should be better dressed for one thing. As it is, they look very pale, almost as though they are consumptive. Let me have a word with them.'

She left me leaning against a tree and walked directly towards the children. As she did so, they turned and hurried away from her. After a few minutes' searching, she came back to me.

'That's the funniest thing,' she exclaimed. 'They ran off, and by the time I got there they'd vanished. Well, no doubt I'll see them around. Maybe somebody in Howtown or Martindale or Pooley Bridge will know who they are. I'd like to get them some warmer clothes.'

I wondered about the children, though I said nothing to Rose. Octavia said she saw a pale face at an upstairs window. Was it possible these children, who might have been vagrants of some kind, Romanies perhaps, had found a way into the house, seeking shelter and warmth? Was it they who left the light on for Rose to see?

We continued our walk. After weeks of bed rest, the cold air came as a shock. I was getting some exercise, but not the robust kind I had been used to. As we reached the lake, we saw that the water had frozen over from bank to bank. Ullswater is a narrow lake, nine miles long but only three wide, so I imagine the ice runs all the way along.

'One year we came down for Christmas and there was ice just like this,' I said. 'I went skating with a friend from Glenridding. We went out every day of the holiday, and it was still frozen when we left.'

'Where was Octavia?'

'She was very small, and her asthma kept her away. Do you think this herbalist can help?'

'I'm sure of it. But don't tell Dr Raverat. He's very agin natural healing.'

'But you're a nurse. Don't you have problems with it?'

'With a lot of it, yes – be careful there, there's a pothole – but I've known some who are helped greatly with herbs.'

I stopped and looked out over the lake.

'God, what I'd give to skate again.'

She squeezed my arm.

'If you work at it, you'll be skating by Christmas, if there's any ice left by then. My only worry would be to make sure the ice wasn't going to break. If that happened you could be in serious trouble, and I doubt very much I could get you out. Now, I think it's time to get you back.'

'What about staying to supper?' I asked.

She shook her head.

'I have to get back to my mother. I've told her all about you. She likes to hear about my patients. I've asked her to come down to visit you some day, but she seems nervous about something and says she'd rather meet you in Pooley Bridge once you're able to get there. She lived down here in Martindale before I was born. She says she knows this stretch of the woods well, knows your house too.'

'Is that why she won't come? What does she know about the house?'

'She won't say. She may know something, she may not. They're all the same round here, they like mysteries, well-hidden secrets, things only a handful of them know. Treating patients is murder. Half the time they won't say what's really going on, they keep back symptoms, they even lie about them. My mother's as bad as the next. All this rain and mist makes the lake people wary of letting the outside world in on their secrets.'

'But I'm not the outside world. My family own this house . . .'

'For the folk round here you're an interloper, however many houses you may own.'

'And what about you?' I asked.

'I'm one of them, but the time I spent training opened my eye. You can't keep secrets and be a nurse, not a lot anyway.'

'Are you keeping any secrets from me?'

'I think we should get back,' she said, and we started to pick our way along the uneven ground. I was gaining my balance, but I didn't want to tell that to Rose. I enjoyed having her by my side, the feel of her hand on my arm. I won't say this to anyone, but I think even more that I am falling in love with her, and I know there's nothing I can do about it.

We both looked up as we reached the front door, to see if there was any sign of life upstairs; but nothing stirred. Perhaps it had, after all, been a trick of the light.

Octavia came to see me safely in. Rose made to go, then turned and smiled.

'I'm sorry I was hard on you earlier.' Saying which she leaned forward and kissed me on the cheek. Hours later, and I can still feel the touch of her lips on my skin.

Octavia had prepared enough for an early meal. But as I entered, I detected something amiss with her. It was already dark, and the candles and lamps had been lit, perhaps more than was really necessary. We ate in silence, something that rarely happened between us. When I got into bed, wrapped in an eiderdown against the cold, she sat down facing me. Her face showed concern, as it had yesterday.

'What's up?' I asked.

She shrugged.

I asked it again, this time using my hands.

She shrugged again.

'Something is wrong,' I said. 'Have you been upstairs again?'

51

This time she shook her head.

'Then what is it? Please don't hold things back from me.'

'It will only worry you,' she said, clenching her jaws and putting her hands back together tightly. I am familiar with this behaviour. When Octavia wants to be difficult, nothing will budge her. We did not speak for the rest of the evening. After my exertions I wanted an early night. Octavia would not sleep without the candles, and I let her keep them.

'But you can't do this every night,' I said. 'Candles and oil are like gold-dust nowadays, and if we use too many we'll have none at all in a week or two.'

'I don't want to sleep in the dark,' she said.

'Why not?'

'Because somebody's living in this house. I heard them earlier. Whispering. When I turned round there was no one there. But there was still whispering.'

Friday, 13 December

I settled Octavia, who fell asleep soon afterwards in spite of her fears, but I found I could not get to sleep myself. I had a nagging pain from my stump, and remained awake until an hour or so before dawn. All night I listened for the whispers Octavia had told me about, but I heard nothing. It didn't make sense, given how very deaf she is. I can't think of anything loud enough for her to hear that I couldn't hear much more clearly. But as long as I stayed awake, the house was silent.

Octavia said nothing about the whispers this morning, and I decided not to raise the subject myself. If the whispering does persist, I may take her back to London to visit her specialist, Dr Radley, just to see if anything is happening to her ears.

I put this to Rose this afternoon, when she turned up to take me for another circuit. She didn't think it likely that a child of Octavia's age would be experiencing changes in the structure of her eardrum, but she did not rule it out entirely. She brought a bottle of herbal medicine. Octavia found the taste disgusting, but Rose used some of our precious sugar to sweeten it, and it went down well.

Our walk went well. We didn't see the four children from yesterday. Rose said she'd asked here and there about them, but nobody knew who they were. I found it easier to lean on my left leg, and almost imagined I could walk without the crutches.

'You will do in time,' Rose said. 'But don't run before you can walk.'

We were finding it easier in one another's company. Rose told me the story of how she had come to train as a nurse. While at school in Glenridding, she had entertained all sorts of ideas as to the course of her future life. Childish dreams of becoming a ballerina or a concert pianist gave way bit by bit to expectations of a husband and a life in a country cottage as a housewife. Of course, the choice of a man in the countryside for a woman like Rose was not exactly wide. There were farmers' sons whom she met at the county shows, and older men who had been farming their acre of land for a decade or more, and the doctor's son, whom she considered far above her, though she knew he liked her. They walked out together for a little while, and one night he kissed her, and she kissed him back, but there was no spark in it, and they drew apart and he went to university and never returned.

'It was his loss,' I said. 'He'll never find anyone as beautiful as you again.'

She stopped and looked into my eyes, giving me a very cheeky look.

'So, you think I'm beautiful, do you?'

'I'm not sure,' I said. 'I'll have to think about it.'

'Well, you're not a bad-looking fellow. Six out of ten, I'd say.'

'Are nurses supposed to engage in banter like this?'

She shook her head.

'We're not. But there's no Sister and no Matron for about fifty miles in any direction, so I do as I please.'

'Is that why you became a nurse? Just so you could mock the rules and regulations.'

She laughed.

'I'm sure you broke a few of those when you were in the Navy.'

'You were telling me why you became a nurse, but so far we've only heard about farmers' sons.'

Her face shifted. The mischief went out of her eyes.

'You're right,' she said, 'I did promise to tell you.'

We walked on a bit in silence. The cold air bit our ears and turned our lips blue. It bit into my wound, exacerbating the pain there. Rose was planning to reduce my morphia another notch.

'I have a brother, Jack,' she said. 'He is five years older than me, and I always remember him being so far ahead. The older I got, the more I appreciated him. My parents adored him. He was bright, and Mother had hopes of a scholarship that would take him to university. She would talk about Cambridge or Oxford in hushed tones. Father talked about driving us all there one day, to one of them at least. Jack was the family's hope for the future, and my hope too, because I felt things couldn't go wrong for me if they went well for him. We went everywhere together, and in the spring and summer we had a little place where we went swimming. We made one another the finest Christmas presents and tied them up with cloth and special string with bows, and one year he bought me a box of face powder in Woolworth's.'

She stopped talking, remembering.

'I still have the box,' she said and fell silent for a minute.

'What happened?' I asked, because I knew something had.

'One day he went with his friends to play football. It's all it was, a silly football game. He was eighteen and had sat his exams and was waiting for the results. My mother knew it had happened before he got home. She went white and sat down, half fainting, and when I brought her a glass of spirits to revive her, she turned to me and said "I can see three men, they're bringing your brother Jack", and not long passed after that when I saw three men coming holding a door, and on the door was Jack, and they told me he'd fallen in the game when someone tackled him, and couldn't stand up on his feet again. We got him to bed and my father fetched the doctor, and the next day our doctor brought another doctor, so we knew something serious was wrong, because Jack could feel nothing beneath the waist and couldn't walk. I was in floods of tears and my mum too, we howled like banshees from morning to night just looking at him, just watching him lie on that bed immobile. They took him in the end to North Lonsdale Hospital, and he's there to this day. He can talk and all that, but it's not the old Jack. I felt terrible in the early days, because I didn't know how to look after him. I wanted to care for him, and after he was taken to the hospital I saw how real nurses did that. That was when I decided to become a nurse. Now, I can do more than pity him. I can help somebody like you to walk. You've had a tremendous blow, but it's not the end of the world like it was for my brother. He passed his exams, you know, he could have had a scholarship. One of the Cambridge colleges was willing to pay him a bursary.

'Before the war is over, you'll just be one of thousands who've lost a limb or an eye or suffered burns across their whole bodies. I've seen men with burns who look like nothing human. But you're still a very good-looking man. Don't take my word for it. By the time you're on your feet, women will be desperate to make your acquaintance. Now, before your head's too stuffed with grand ideas and you start to have mad thoughts about my finding you attractive, we'd better walk on a bit further.'

Somehow, knowing about Jack makes it easier for me to understand why she pushes me to make an effort. There's nothing she can do for her brother, she says, for he will never walk again, short of a miracle. Every time she can help somebody like myself, it's a compensation for the state her brother is in.

As for her compliment about being a good-looking man, I'm sure she says that to all her patients, men and women alike, choosing her words carefully in every case. For all that, it did lift my spirits. I can't think of anyone I would rather hear compliments from. She may be teasing me within an inch of my life, but I'm in a mood to be teased. By Rose, that is; I won't let anyone else pull my leg. Goodness, what have I just written? I need to clear this leg business out of my head.

Saturday, 14 December

We have only just had breakfast, but I need to write this down. Last night something strange happened. About three in the morning I was wakened by a shrill scream. It was Octavia, screaming loudly – something she has never done in her life before. I calmed her and the screaming stopped.

'What's wrong?' I asked.

56

She signed to me, her hands shaking.

'I had a bad dream,' she said. 'There were children in it. Four children. They came down from the attic. I knew they were dead.'

'But we don't have an attic,' I said.

She looked at me.

'We did,' she said. 'Above the rooms upstairs.'

'How do you know?'

'Because the children told me.'

'What were these children like?'

'They were very pale. There were three girls my age and an older boy.'

'What did they want with you? Did they say?'

'They want me to join them.'

She said nothing more, but she would not go back to sleep.

Monday, 16 December

Rose arrived today with Mrs Mathewman, the witch doctor. I call her that because I distrust anything superstitious or occult, be it holy healers or holy places or medicines or fairies at the bottom of someone's garden.

I have only allowed this woman in because it pleases Rose to bring her, and I will do almost anything for Rose, though I have known her for only a very short time. She was here on Saturday and again on Sunday, although she had no need to come, and I'm sure she has plenty of other patients to see to. She told me she had attended church service at St Peter's in Martindale on the way to see me, and she overheard a plan to put up a window in memory of over one thousand men who drowned in the sinking of HMS *Glorious* in Norwegian waters earlier this year. She wants me to come to church with her next week, and I've said what it seems right to say, to keep her happy, though in truth I have never been much of a believer. I may go with her at Christmas and sing carols and admire their nativity. I find it odd that she is an active churchgoer, especially in a time of war, when I have lost my faith in man.

As I have said before, I am falling in love with Rose, and even though I know there can be no future in it, I cannot steady my heart or its trembling when I set eyes on her, the agitation when she is not around.

But I'm rushing ahead. I haven't yet said a word about what happened. Rose got me up and into an armchair, and we stayed in the living room all the time. Mrs Mathewman took Octavia off to the sun room, where we used to sit and look at the lake across a vista made by cutting down some trees at the front of the house. I don't know what they talked about: afterwards, Octavia refused to say what it was. All she would say was that it was 'private'. She was given a second bottle of medicine, one more palatable to a child, and searched out a spoon to administer it to herself.

Mrs Mathewman came as a surprise to me. She did not look remotely like a witch or any other being with claims to supernatural powers. She was well dressed and softly spoken, with little trace of an accent. Rose later told me that she had been to university, to Newnham College, Cambridge and studied like a man, except that they won't let women have full degrees. She's not a great beauty perhaps, but not what I had expected. And she is clearly intelligent.

She told me what she had made of Octavia's asthma, and assured me her remedies could improve it, maybe even banish it for good. I nodded and said 'of course, of course', or feigned surprise with a string of 'surely nots'. To be honest, I wasn't overly enthusiastic, but the woman made a good impression on me. That is, until she changed the subject.

She got up to take her leave, then sat down again hesitantly. Her confident manner deserted her, as if she was having second thoughts about what she'd just been saying. A shadow seemed to cross her face.

'Lieutenant,' she said, 'I hope you will forgive me if I raise another matter. Octavia told me one or two things that are troubling me. She says you might not like her having told me, that you are a sceptic. I understand that. My years at university taught me the importance of a sceptical attitude. But I'm not a sceptic through and through like you. I've come to realize that there are realities that fall between the grids and cages we make for ourselves. I studied mathematics and came top of my year, beating men as well as other women. I am a scientist, but I have learned to keep an open mind.

'Octavia told me she heard sounds in the living room when you were out with Rose, and that she feels uneasy about the upstairs rooms. She is not, I think, an imaginative child. After she had her medicine, when she went to talk to you, I slipped upstairs. I went into a few rooms, then I came down again. Mr Lancaster, allow me to speak to you honestly. There is something in your house. That's as clear as I can be at the moment. I don't know what it is or what it wants, but I can say that it is an evil force. I felt it immediately on climbing your stairs. This house is harbouring something wicked, and I believe that if you stay here it must destroy you in the end. You and Octavia and, if she is here, Rose too. If you care about Octavia and Rose then you have to act. Go back to London, Lieutenant, and leave this house to itself.'

I stopped her with a simple gesture.

'Mrs Mathewman, I'm grateful for your consideration, but now I'd like to ask you to leave. I don't want to hear more about this "something". I'd like you to leave, and I don't want you to come back. If Octavia thrives on your remedy, I'm sure Nurse Sansom can pick up a fresh bottle as she did before. You'll be paid properly. I'm grateful for all you're doing for her, but I don't want to see her upset more than she is. Some brisk walks in the cold air will get these nightmares out of her system.'

She said nothing until we reached the door. As she made to leave, she turned back.

'If there are further disturbances, don't hesitate to call me. I will do what I can to help.'

Tuesday, 17 December

The weather has improved. The ice on the lake has melted like snow on a hot roof, though there is talk of worse weather to come. Rose came to me as usual, and I did not dare ask her how she managed to be so regular with me when she must have so many other patients for fear of awakening her conscience and leading her to choose to be with me only one day in seven, one day in ten, or worse. Without her, I cannot think how I would go on.

We took advantage of the milder weather. It was almost forty degrees outside, warm enough to melt ice, but still extremely cold. We wrapped up warmly as before. She held me at first, being unsure how soft the ground might be, but I soon settled into a way of walking that let me place increasing pressure on my stump. I found that my artificial limb had been soundly made, and I came more and more to rely on it as I walked.

We found a path along the lake. I remembered it from my

childhood. That made me think of the house, and the fact that we had never had talk of hauntings or ghostly noises until Octavia arrived. I did not think her mischievous. Quite the opposite. But I realized that coming all the way out here had placed a strain on her. She is completely deaf, and at home she can only respond to any of the family or servants by being right in front of them and able to read their lips. For the most part, life here is silent, and when she leaves the house she walks in silence until she reaches Howtown, where she has become something of a pet to the villagers. I fancy her brain is compensating for this loneliness by implanting sounds, in the way someone else might experience hallucinations.

As we walked, Rose slipped her arm through mine, and it was no longer a hand clasping me in order to steady my steps, but a gesture of affection, or so I let myself fancy.

'Dominic, there's something I need to talk with you about,' she said. 'I think you know what it is.'

'Mrs Mathewman,' I said.

'She tells me you have forbidden her to enter your house again. Of course, it's none of my business, but I did bring her here and I asked her to treat Octavia, so I feel responsible. And I'm worried in case word of this episode should get back to the hospital. They would turn me out the moment there was any suspicion I'd brought in a herbalist.'

'There's no need to worry about that,' I said. 'You acted quite honourably. I'm still interested to see what her remedy does, if it does anything. Herbs are material substances. I don't rule out the possibility that they can have material effects. They used willow bark to relieve pain many centuries before we had it as aspirin. If Mrs Mathewman's concoction can improve Octavia's breathing, I'll go along with it. But as you know, I'm a sceptic in these matters. And that's why I won't have her in the house again. Did she tell you that she's been encouraging Octavia in her belief that she hears thing here? She even warned me that there's something in the house, though she wouldn't tell me exactly what she meant by "something". Octavia is a sensitive child, as I'm sure you've noticed, and someone like Mrs Mathewman could have a profound effect on her, for she seems a very admirable and confident woman. If she's going to put ideas into Octavia's head, I can't tolerate that.'

'Very well. I'll explain this to her. I'm sure you're right, and it's right of you to be concerned about Octavia. It's a shame this has happened. She's an intelligent woman and it's a pity you can't talk with her more. She's a mine of information on any number of topics. Most of it's far above my head, of course. She knows a lot about this district and the Lakes in general. History, ancient customs: things like that.'

I left it at that, not wanting to reawaken whatever negative emotions my banning Mrs Mathewman might have caused for Rose. Rose says she will take me to the North Lonsdale Hospital for an examination.

'I'll see if I can get an appointment in a week or two. It's not that I don't trust Dr Raverat, but the Lonsdale has a specialist in your sort of trauma, and I'm surprised you weren't taken to see him as soon as you arrived there.'

'You know I depend on you for everything,' I said.

'I realize that. But it's not healthy for a patient to grow excessively fond of his nurse or to depend on her for everything. We shall have to find a way to wean you off me, Lieutenant.' My heart sank when she said this.

We walked a little further. Near the path and down among the winter-bare trees, plants of a hundred varieties lay dormant. Wood sage and wood sorrel, golden saxifrage and marsh marigold lay waiting, curled and pale for spring. A part of me had sincerely hoped there would be no spring, or that I should not set eyes on the next. But my feelings for Rose have changed all that.

'I used to sail round here,' I said. 'All the nine miles from the bottom to the top.'

'Were you good?' Rose asked.

'Of course I was,' I said, grinning.

'I imagine you were. You must have had years of practice.'

'My father taught me. We've always been a sailing family. Until now, that is.'

'Why stop now?'

'Surely you know the answer to that,' I exclaimed, more harshly than I had intended.

'Actually,' she said, 'I think you and I are about to have our second argument. But you aren't the first and you won't be the last to take this attitude. Yes, you're disabled. But I'll have no sympathy with you if you claim you can't do this or that because of your disability. You've proved that you can walk, and I know you'll walk better as time goes by. You may not be able to kick a ball round a football pitch or join the local rugby team. But you'll be able to play some gentle tennis, and in the next few days you're going to take me and Octavia for a sail up and down Lake Ullswater.'

I froze at the thought, but she wouldn't take 'no' for an answer.

We turned and started to walk back. The light was falling, and in the woods a darkness full of shadows lurked among the trees. I felt a tremor passed through me. Could Mrs Mathewman have been telling the truth, could there be something in the house?

We were almost there when we saw the four children again, standing in what seemed to be the same spot, and looking at the house. As we came near them, I decided I must speak to them.

They were looking at me, and a chill went through me, for they all turned and looked at exactly the same moment, as though guided by a single thought. Their faces seemed livid as before. I smiled in an attempt to disarm them. Rose came behind me, a smile on her face as well. But as I drew close, the children ran off into the woods and were swallowed up in seconds by the darkness. I called after them, but no one answered.

We continued to the house. My sour mood was beginning to lift as my fancy played with the pleasures of sailing on the lake, even in winter, and above all with the thought of sailing with Rose and showing her the paces of the *Firefly*. I would try and go to the yacht club in the morning and remove the dust sheets. Perhaps Rose was right. Perhaps I could sail again.

She stayed again for supper. Her bicycle panniers were stuffed with food saved from her rations.

'I can't let you feed me,' she said. 'Your allowance won't stretch to guests. But what I've brought should let us all have a feast.'

She had brought eggs and ham and tins of baked beans, and it dawned on me that a district nurse must come in for her fair share of 'extras' passed on by grateful patients.

'I'm sorry the baked beans are the new type,' she said.

I creased my brow.

'I hadn't known there was a new type.'

'While you were away, they took the piece of pork out of the tins.'

'Another reason to be angry with Herr Hitler.'

Octavia seemed well and over our meal declared that her breathing had improved.

'You've not been outside yet,' I said. 'That will be the test.'

'I liked Mrs Mathewman,' she said. 'When will she come again?'

I fudged and said it was too early to tell.

Octavia went to bed early. Rose and I sat in the kitchen, listening to the radio. The news items weren't very uplifting. Most of the bulletin was taken up with a report on the two-hundredth bombing of Liverpool. It's hard to believe they are going through such devastation. But after that we cheered up a bit listening to the latest hit recordings. They played 'Fools Rush In' by Tony Martin, that Ink Spots song, 'When the Swallows Come Back to Capistrano' (though neither Rose nor I has a clue where Capistrano is). She has a soft spot for Cliff Edwards singing 'When You Wish upon a Star'.

When it was time to leave, she bent over and kissed me on the cheek as before. This time, I tried to kiss her back, and for a moment she let me, and it seemed as if our little kisses would turn into something more serious. But she stepped away with a serious look on her face, then smiled and said 'I'm sorry, D . . . Dominic. I . . . It's too fast. And it's not simple. Let's stay friends as long as we can.'

She left almost at once, and I cursed myself for having been such an idiot. I'd blown it. Or, it struck me, it was more likely my leg had ruined it for me.

When I got to bed, I found Octavia awake and waiting for me, a candle burning next to her. I am growing worried about her. She has no friends to play with, something that I had hoped might happen to sustain her new life in the country. She has lost some of the sparkle I've talked about before. I haven't heard her laugh once since we got here. And it's getting worse. She seems to be taking on a new personality, as if the house is weighing on her, as if our remoteness here has drained her of that buoyant spirit I've always known her to be famous for.

'Not asleep?' I asked.

'No. I want to talk to you.'

To help me see her better, I lit two lamps and brought them across.

'This sounds serious,' I said, fearing she might have been hearing things again.

'I don't think so,' she said. 'It sounds good to me.'

The lamplight threw the movements of her hands into long shadows that criss-crossed the room. It was cold, and our breath hung on the air. She looked comfortable in her little bed.

'Did you make a hot water bottle for yourself?' I asked, feeling guilty that I hadn't prepared one for her.

She nodded.

'So, what is this about?'

She smiled.

'I heard a voice,' she said. 'It was a message for you.'

'You mean, there was somebody in here with you . . .'

'Let me finish. There was nobody here, but I heard the voice quite clearly.'

'You mean you imagined it.'

She shook her head.

'The voice was real. Do you want me to go on, or would you rather I just shut up and not tell you? If you want to know, it was a message. A message for you.'

'You mean, a message from the dead? Is that what you think this voice was?'

'I don't know.'

She was straining now, using her voice to make explosive sounds I could make no sense of.

'Very well,' I said. 'Tell me the message.'

She calmed down and took some deep breaths. I hoped this exchange would not bring on an asthma attack.

'It's not a long message,' she said. 'It's from someone called

Billy Morgan. He says you're not to worry about him any more. He's not cold now. He's anxious you should know this.'

She stopped talking and looked directly at me, her face wreathed in shadows. I thought my heart would stop beating or that my eyes would close and I would fall unconscious to the floor and that the world would close about me. But I rallied. She could not possibly have known anything about Billy Morgan. I had never mentioned him to her or to anyone else since my rescue from the *Resolution*. Straight away, I resolved to say nothing to Octavia to confirm his existence or his death.

Billy was a Welsh naval lieutenant I had known on board the *Hotspur*. He and I had been transferred together to the *Resolution* and had become firm friends. He used to complain about the cold when we were up in the Arctic. After the sinking of the *Resolution*, while I was in the *Aba* and later in hospital, I had asked repeatedly about him, hoping he'd been brought to either place, imagining he was in the next ward. But when the names of survivors were passed round, he wasn't on the list. I had never given up hope that he might turn up somewhere, but now an innocent child had dashed those hopes for ever.

Outside, a wind had risen through the evening. Our silence was taken up by it, by its blows and flurries, its alarms and whistles.

'Dominic,' she said, though I was hardly listening. 'Why are you crying? I thought it was good news.'

I nodded. The wind howled and the shadows in the room danced. For the first time, I knew there was indeed something in the house. And it wasn't Billy Morgan or even a seabed full of the dead.

'Yes,' I said, 'thank you. It was good news, but it was also sad.'

And she said nothing, and I said nothing more, and the wind went on blowing, and the shadows went on with their strange

Morris dance, like the dancers in Bacup who process on Easter Sunday with blackened faces. I thought of Billy Morgan, and I thought of Rose, and I wondered what she had meant when she said things were moving too fast.

I did not sleep until late, and when I did I dreamed of dancers dancing on silent feet, and when I looked they had black faces like the Bacup Morrismen. But without eyes, nose or mouth, and some danced on bleeding stumps and others in shoes of old leather, and drums played very near, and they waved their bleeding hands in the air, jingling and jangling little copper bells. In each hand they carried sticks that they beat together against themselves and against each other, in time with the drums. I can still see them, even though I am awake, and I can still hear their bells and sense the soft dancing of their stumps on a floor of beaten earth. If Billy Morgan can still find me here and pass on a message from beyond his watery grave, what else is possible? Do the dancers dance their way here from Glenridding or Pooley Bridge, are they men of Howtown or Martindale, are they living men or dead? And does Billy Morgan dance among them with a face eaten away by little fishes, does he live upstairs from Octavia and myself, in the unlit bedrooms of this house?

More disturbingly, one thought comes to me, that the *Resolution* was hit amidships and sank at once, taking all hands with her, and that I am as dead as Billy Morgan and the rest of the crew. My body is at the bottom of the sea, but my spirit walks this house, where it has conjured up a vision of female beauty and fallen in love with her. Is that what the dead do? Make hell

68

and heaven as they please, shut themselves away where no one can find them?

Rose did not turn up yesterday, but she came knocking on the door early this morning, as planned. She smiled when Octavia let her in and smiled at me when she found me, still in bed. Octavia beetled off to play with a jigsaw I had found in a dining-room cupboard.

'You're very early,' I said. 'I've not had breakfast yet.'

'I have a free day,' she said. 'Marjory Wainright is on duty at Dr Raverat's today, so I thought I'd come to see you for some walking and some sailing, if that's all right. Though looking at you tucked up in there like a bug in a rug, I don't know that climbing in there with you might not be the better option.'

'I don't think I could control myself,' I said, making the remark light.

'Don't worry. You wouldn't be the only one. We're all human underneath, Dominic.'

'Some of us more than others, I think,' I said, still trying to retain the light mood.

'I think,' she said, and I could detect some nervousness in her voice, nervousness that wasn't usually there, 'I think you're the most human man I've ever known.'

'Me?' I was genuinely surprised, and I couldn't really understand what she was getting at. 'I'm not even complete.'

'I don't mean bodily, though I think you do look very well. I mean as a person, inside.'

'But I'm a wreck. I'm not handling my life very well. I'm sure you must be well fed up with me by now.'

'Quite the contrary. And I'm sorry for what I said two days ago, about you going too fast. These things will take their own course at their own speed.'

I looked at her without blinking for what seemed an age.

'What do you mean "these things"?'

'I mean affairs of the heart. You probably haven't noticed yet, but we're having one. It's not up to much yet, but it will pick up speed. When I said I'd like to climb into bed with you, that's exactly what I meant.'

I stared at her.

'Women don't . . .'

'You'd be surprised what women think. The war is changing things. Nobody has time to wait these days. A man goes off to war and is killed, never to come home. People are marrying in droves, and who can blame them? Some couples have one night for their honeymoon, then he goes off to his train or boat or plane the following morning and she never sees him again. It's our turn now, or it will be soon. You won't go to war again, and I doubt there'll be bombs on Howtown, but none of our lives is certain.'

'Are you saying that you love me? I won't believe any of this if you don't tell me in as many words.'

She came beside me, and most unexpectedly I felt myself quickening beneath the sheets, then she leaned over and kissed me, and the kiss grew deeper until there seemed to be no 'you' and no 'I'. I moved to touch her, but she pulled away, and I could see she was red and flustered.

'I love you,' she said.

'I've loved you since the minute I set eyes on you,' I answered.

'Oh, I know that,' she said. 'Women always know.'

'Won't you kiss me again?'

She grinned.

'We have to ration everything nowadays. If I did kiss you, I'd be in bed with you before you could fight me off, then Octavia would finish her jigsaw and come in to say hullo, and . . .'

At the moment, Octavia appeared, as if on cue.

'Rose, are you any good at jigsaw puzzles?'

I interpreted and Rose nodded.

'Later,' she said.

Octavia looked crestfallen.

'Oh, please,' she said. 'Just help me get this started. It has two thousand pieces.'

'What is it?' Rose asked.

'I don't know. A picture. Some painting. By a man called Alma.'

I laughed and shook my head.

'It's a painting of ancient Rome by Alma-Tadema,' I said, making a different configuration of my fingers to spell the name, just as she had done. 'I used to make it up in the holidays. You'll like it when it's finished.'

'I'll come and help you now. But no more than half an hour.'

'All right.' Octavia smiled broadly and made to go. As she reached the door, she turned back.

'When are you two getting married?' she asked, as if nothing was more beyond doubt. The looks on our faces must have been a treat.

'What makes you think we might be planning to get married?'

'Your friend Billy told me, of course. He knows a lot of things. And Rose's lipstick is smeared, which means you've been kissing, and I can see red on your lips as well, Dominic.'

'Can you hear Billy now?' I asked.

She shook her head.

'Billy's gone,' she said. 'He says he's afraid to stay here, that there's something here that frightens him. He wouldn't tell me what it is.'

'Octavia,' said Rose, 'I think it will be better if we go to the dining room and take a look at this jigsaw of yours. I need to dress Dominic's leg, so we must get on.'

71

While Rose helped Octavia with her jigsaw I managed to get out of bed and to dress myself without help. Aided by my crutches, I went to the kitchen and made myself some bacon and eggs. Bacon is like gold dust nowadays, with four ounces each a week, as much as I used to eat in a day. Rose's eggs have come in very handy indeed. By the time I finished, I was still hungry.

Rose came in while I was putting things away. In order to hold things, I found I was hopping more than walking. She took over and told me to sit down. When she was done and she had washed and dried the dishes, she sat down opposite me.

'Who's Billy?' she asked, and I detected a note of worry in her voice. 'Or perhaps I should say "Who *was* Billy?" '

I answered as best I could.

'She only told me two nights ago,' I finished.

'And you think she's telling the truth? There's no other way she could have known about him?'

I shook my head.

'I never spoke of him to her, nor to anyone else. I'd have mentioned him to you, but I still feel choked up about him.'

'Could you have spoken about him in your sleep?'

'Perhaps. I've no way of knowing. All I see in my sleep at present are Morris dancers with black faces and stumps for legs. Even if I had talked about him, she couldn't have heard me. She needs to see my lips or the gestures I make with my hands.'

'But Hilary Mathewman says there is something in this house, something very dark. Octavia said earlier that she's been hearing things, a girl who until now could hear barely anything. And now she puts her finger on the one person who is dead and close to you and wants to tell you he's all right. However much a rationalist you may be, Dominic, none of your rationalizations will add up to this.'

'Then what will add up?'

'I don't know. It's just possible that something is unblocking Octavia's hearing, though she may not know what sounds are really like.'

I thought about this carefully, then shook my head.

'It still doesn't add up. Even if she has started hearing sounds, she doesn't understand language. If I tell you what she says, it's just an approximation.'

'And yet she claims to understand. You're back to square one, Dominic. If she can't grasp language, how can she understand a name like "Billy Morgan" or the message she says he gave to her?'

This all made me uneasy. Anyone else might have angered me, by making me see how inadequate my arguments were, but Rose could have told me black was white and I would have nodded and said "Amen".'

'Let's go to the yacht club,' I said. 'If the weather's holding up, we'll try to get the *Firefly* up and running.'

Friday, 20 December

Christmas is just days away. We had a letter from my parents saying they can't get hold of enough petrol to do the journey up and back. Tomorrow brings the darkest night. Each day as it closes in brings thicker shadows. I begin to imagine things, impossible things. I wonder if it will not bring madness.

Yesterday continued on a magical note. Octavia was left to work on her jigsaw. Rose and I walked up to Howtown Bay, where the new yacht club sits next to the steamer landing. It's a big bay, with room for plenty more boats. The *Firefly* is an old XOD–Class twenty-footer keelboat with a wooden hull, a wooden mast, and a wooden rudder at the back, and I love her with passion. She has a cutaway forefoot keel that slices through the water, and she was built for us in 1930 by Kemp and Co. down in Hythe. Before her, we'd sailed on the *Dragonfly*.

She's not one of those large yachts that force the captain to be up on deck, running and jumping. There's a little well that seats two people. Rose had never set foot on a boat before, save for the Ullswater steamers, so I told her to sit quietly and watch everything I did. Finding her out of her element like that renewed my confidence, and I unmoored *Firefly* into a stiff breeze that moved us quickly into the lake. Without my leg, I found it hard to keep my balance at first, but before long we were sailing perfectly. The artificial leg took whatever pressure I put on it, and though it hurt quite badly at times, the dose of morphia Rose had given me beforehand settled it down.

I relaxed into all my old sailing habits, and once we were running well with a fresh wind behind us, I let my hand fall to the side and found Rose's hand and held it. She squeezed back, turned once to look at me, then faced forward again. There was no need for words. I find, when I'm sailing with a friend, that words are redundant. All my worries and misgivings vanish. Who has not known that to happen, on open water, with a large sky above: blue or grey, it makes no difference. I had imagined bringing girls out in the *Firefly* before, holding their hands, and kissing them if they let me. Now, holding Rose's hand, I felt more at peace than I ever had before.

We must have stayed out well over an hour. Rose had brought her little Kodak Bantam camera, and took a string of photos, of me, of the boat, of the shore. She didn't think they would turn out well, but I thought the snaps would be a kind of bond between us, shared memories we could look at in years to come. By then, although we had dressed warmly, we were both feeling cold, so I turned at the head of the lake and brought us back down to Howtown. I dropped anchor and stood, thinking how best to get myself ashore. As I stood there, a man in late middle age approached. He wore a blazer and a little captain's cap covered partly in gold thread, the sort no serious sailor would consider wearing. Beneath his nose there sprouted a neatly-trimmed moustache. I had never seen him before.

He barked at me.

'You!' he snapped. 'What's your name?'

'I don't know that that's any of your business,' I answered.

'You don't know what my business is,' he said, still barking, 'and I don't think I care to explain it to you. Just now I demand to know what you're doing out in a pleasure boat with a floozie in tow.'

Behind me, Rose started laughing. I turned and looked at her sternly, but she'd started and couldn't stop.

'What I'm doing is none of your business, and if you'd like to get out of my way, I'd like to get ashore.'

'What damned cheek! Look here, are you a conchie or some-thing? Because I'll see to it you're kicked out of this club, if you're a member, which I doubt. By God, you're a scruffy thing, aren't you? Don't you know there's a war on? We're at war with Jerry, surely even you have heard of that. So why aren't you dressed properly and out on the front lines doing your duty for God, King and country?'

The laughing behind me had ceased. He'd gone too far, from the ridiculous to something more serious. Suddenly, I felt Rose slip past me and jump on to the waterside. Then, without a word, she reached for my hand and helped me get from the *Firefly* to dry land. Without further ado, she bent down and, before I could guess what she was doing, she rolled my trouser leg up to the knee.

75

My self-appointed nemesis began to gurgle.

'He lost his leg at the Battle of Dakar,' she said. 'Now will you please leave and never speak to us again? And if I see you here again, I will not hesitate to throw you in the lake.'

Still mumbling, he took his leave, shambling off towards the small clubhouse. I let him go. The war has frayed tempers. Perhaps he meant well and lacked the resources to express himself properly.

We made sure *Firefly* was tied up safely. Back on land, it seemed warmer. We shivered, then held hands again. It felt as though the day had ended, but it had scarcely begun.

We were walking past Howtown and its sparse habitations. The ferry had just gone. I could still see it, the *Raven*, chugging north towards Pooley Bridge. When I turned back, I noticed Octavia. In one hand she held the basket in which she always put her shopping. But her other hand held that of a girl of about her age. Seeing me, she veered in our direction, bringing her friend with her.

'Dominic, Rose, this is my friend Clare. Say hello.'

She spelled the girl's name with her fingers, then tapped out some Morse code on my palm. I smiled and looked at Clare. She had a patch of rough skin on her left cheek. Wasn't she one of the four children we'd seen before? She was a little shorter than Octavia, with black hair that looked almost grey in the dim light. She wore a coat about two sizes too big for her tiny frame, made of felt – or so it seemed to me – and on her feet were shoes like clogs.

I asked how they had met, and Octavia answered that they had bumped into one another on Octavia's first day here, when she went into Howtown to buy some food.

'Clare says she's an evacuee like me. She's only been here for a month.'

Rose went up close to Clare.

'Hello, Clare. My name's Rose. I don't think I've seen you round here before, though you seem a little familiar.'

'I live on a farm up there,' she said, in a strange, rasping voice. She pointed behind her.

'Really? Is that Hallin Fell? What's the name of the farm?'

'Ravencragg it's called. Ravencragg Farm.'

Rose nodded. 'I've heard the name,' she said. 'But I thought it had been closed down when old Martin Drablow died.'

'Mark Drablow lives there now. I lodge with him.'

'I'll see a health visitor goes out to check on you.'

Rose smiled and seemed about to turn away, then went back to Clare.

'Clare, you do understand that Octavia's deaf, don't you?'

The girl nodded.

'How do you speak to her? You know she can't hear a word you say?'

'She hears me, Miss. I have a little sister like her, she was born that way, and I've learned how to speak to her.'

Rose frowned, though she still smiled as she questioned Clare.

'With your fingers?' she asked. 'Like this?'

She nodded, then turned to Octavia and gestured to her. Octavia smiled back. When Octavia looked at me again, she flashed a message that they had to go, but that she'd be back well before dark.

Rose fumbled in her coat pocket and brought out the Bantam. She still had some exposures left. I remembered that one of the lads on board ship had carried one. I wondered what had happened to him and to the photographs he'd taken. Octavia had brought her Weltini Speed Candid to Ullswater, but so far I hadn't seen her use it. Rose pulled out the front of the Bantam and gestured to the girls that she'd like to take their photograph.

Clare seemed reluctant to pose, as though she had never set eyes on a camera before, but Octavia drew her in while Rose clicked the button. Another shot and she was done. She slipped the camera back in her pocket. I noticed that Clare hadn't smiled once during this exchange. They went on, and Rose took me to the shop cum post office.

'Those were the last two shots,' she said. 'I want to send the film off to get it developed. There's a man in Keswick who does it for tourists. He'll send the snaps back by post.' She wound the film back, took it out and put it in a stout envelope, courtesy of the postmistress. Rose and I headed back to Hallinhag House.

Once there, I lit candles, even though it wouldn't be dark for a while. Rose prepared lunch, and we ate in the kitchen. She had brought some rice from her own rations and added lamb she'd been sent from one of the nearby farms, a meat more readily available in the Lake District than most other parts of the country. There were spices in the cupboard, and with these she created a very tasty curry. We were awkward with one another, now we felt on the verge of becoming lovers. As before, she was cautious of rushing things. I wanted to go to the living room to rest, but the presence of the bed and the implications it held since our brief courtship early that morning inhibited me. I suggested we transfer to the study, where I had always worked as a child. Rose made cups of acorn coffee, added a spoonful each of honey and some powdered milk. It tasted horrible, but at least it was hot.

'What do you make of Clare?' I asked after we sat down.

'She seems malnourished. I'd like to have a chance to examine her. And her clothes all seem old, like hand-me-downs. The farms here don't fare well on the whole, and with the war on they're bound to feel the pinch. Did you notice that she didn't have a local accent? She must be a refugee from another part of the country.'

I nodded agreement.

'If I didn't know better, I'd say her accent was Portuguese. But that doesn't make sense, does it?'

'I found her very serious,' said Rose, 'I don't know about you; and I had a bad feeling about her, something I can't put into words.'

'What sort of bad feeling?'

She shrugged.

'I'd have to speak to her more. Did you see her eyes?'

I nodded.

'Yes, there was a quality, a sort of deadness.'

'That's it. Looking at her eyes, she seems much older than she is. I suspect her upbringing has been cruel. She said nothing about a mother. Could that be it? Is she an orphan with a father who's away all the time?'

'Well, we'll speak to her when we see her again. I'd like to know how she knows deaf language, if she knows very much at all.'

I drank my 'coffee' slowly, spinning out the minutes. Rose hadn't said whether she had to leave soon or not. I showed her my collection of Portuguese stamps, which I'd collected avidly as a boy and abandoned on reaching my teenage years, and which I'd found in the study. The album had remained here in Hallinhag for several years. I have a 100 reis lilac, an 1894 pictorial commemorating Henry the Navigator's birth, and a 1924 stamp that marked the birth of the great poet Luís de Camões. Rose seemed fascinated by them, and came to sit next to me while I browsed through my album.

'Dominic,' she said, 'I hope you don't find me cold. But I find it hard to call you "darling" yet, for I've had no practice at all in such things. I love you very much, though, and I know I'll not change, whatever you may think. We have time ahead of us. The war will finish before long. You won't go on board a ship again. We'll both live through it. When I'm ready, I'll go to bed with you, and when it's time we'll get married.'

'And children after that?'

'Yes, children. All the children you want.'

'Will they be born with one leg?'

'Of course. They'll take after their father in every way, especially the girls.' She lifted my hand and kissed it gently. Then she looked at her nurse's watch and said she had to go, she had an errand to run for her mother.

'I'll try to get back tonight,' she said and bent over and kissed me hard.

'Don't bother coming to the door,' she said. 'Go to bed now and rest.'

I did as she ordered and went to bed with thoughts of her in my heart. But my first dreams of her were chased away by harrowing visions of dancing men without faces. They moved in a stranger dance than before, without legs entirely now, bearing themselves up on their hands yet moving quite as quickly as dancers in a theatre, and in the blackened masks where their faces had been, little eyes appeared. As they turned in a ceaseless procession, the eyes followed me, and I heard lonely music drift down from a bleak hill that towered over us all, and when I looked up beyond the hill, at the sky, I could see planes forging through the heavens, bombers accompanied by fighters, and the bombers bombed the hill so that it fell apart and fell down to cover the dancing men. The music grew in volume, and the aeroplanes flew away, and the dancers began to claw their way back out of the soil. Once they were free, they began to dance again, on their legs this time, and I noticed four children among them, their faces blackened, their legs just bone. I woke sweating and lay in bed for a long time. Is there something wrong with me, or is it the house?

Octavia returned just before sunset. She had left Clare behind in Howtown, she said, because she had to go to the farm and help. Mr Drablow was busier than ever with the war, she told me.

'What about her mother?' I asked.

Octavia shook her head.

'Dead,' she said, crossing her two index fingers to indicate a grave. 'Some disease, years ago.'

I would have stayed in bed without supper and gone to sleep, for I was still tired from my morning exertions; but the thought of Rose's return that evening encouraged me to stay awake. I got up, put on my new leg, and made my way to the study, where I had books to read. My time in the Navy had given me very few opportunities in which to bury myself in books, but it was a great pleasure I had always pursued from about the age of twelve, and I resented the time I had lost. I had started to wonder whether, when the war was ended and my ability to walk complete, I might take examinations and go to university to study something useful. But I as quickly remembered that, by then, I would be married to Rose and would need a trade to bring in money once she gave up work to be a full-time housewife. Of course, the family could well afford to pay my way to a degree. But would my father see that as anything but a total waste of money? If I want money of my own, I'll just have to join the firm and give up thoughts of anything else.

I'm reading an American novel that came out this year. My mother bought it for me in London, and I brought it here. It's called *The Ox-Bow Incident* and it tells the story of a lynch mob and the crime they commit by hanging three innocent men. It's a kind of Western, but I'm enjoying it all the same. My father has no time for Westerns.

Octavia banged the gong to call me to the dining room to eat supper, a trout each with green vegetables, but no potatoes. Maybe next time. The trout was fresh and delicious, and I found enough salt to flavour it.

Later

It's midnight and I'm in the study, but I'm not reading, nor do I have any wish to read. What happened a few hours ago has shaken me. It has shaken Rose as well. She is staying here tonight, for she will not cycle back for love nor money. It is not the journey that disturbs her, but being alone in the dark, with no company but the lake. She reached here about eight o'clock and brought some chocolate and tiny cakes. Octavia went to bed, and Rose and I went to the study, where I sat on my chair and she on the little sofa my mother had insisted on placing there some years earlier. We ate the chocolate. She'd saved up her ration of four ounces a week for three weeks and travelled to Penrith with Dr Raverat to get some. A patient had given her a present of several ounces of tea, and we made a pot, added powdered milk and half a teaspoon of sugar each. My supply of sugar will soon be gone, but Rose says she may be able to find some.

About ten o'clock, Octavia came to the study. She was sleepy-eyed, and stood in her lemon night-dress, wringing her hands in front of her.

'What's wrong, dear?' I asked.

'I want you to speak to Clare,' she said.

'Of course. What about?'

'She won't let me sleep. None of them will let me sleep.'

'Who are "them"?'

'Haven't you seen them?' she asked. 'There's Clare and her three friends, Adam, Helen and Margaret.'

Rose looked at me meaningfully. I knew what she was thinking.

'Octavia,' she asked, 'how are they stopping you from sleeping?'

'Because they keep whispering. I know I can't hear, but I can hear them whispering.'

'When you're outside with them, you mean?'

She shook her head.

'No, not outside. In here. They come here and whisper, and sometimes they say things out loud. Frightening things, things I don't want to hear. I don't know how I understand them, but I do understand them. And I can hear them dancing and beating sticks like fencing.'

'But they're not here,' I said. 'They live somewhere else.'

She inhaled deeply, steadying herself.

'No,' she said, 'that's where you're wrong. They live in this house. I think they're dead. I think Clare is dead. I think they all died a long time ago.'

'But surely you can't hear them now,' I countered. My skin was crawling. All the blood had drained from Rose's face.

'Of course I can. They're here with us right this moment. Can't you see?'

I was about to ask her where they were when I looked at Rose and saw her staring rigidly at a spot somewhere behind me. I turned my swivel chair. At first I could see nothing but shadows. Then the shadows parted and I saw them. The four children I had twice seen outside, Clare among them. Their mouths were wide open, and I could hear them hissing like geese, and they were very pale and their clothes were covered in a layer of dust and their hair was matted and coarse. I thought Octavia was right. I thought they were dead. I thought they were old and dead and dusty and pale. I thought their eyes looked at me and Rose and Octavia like eyes that had seen the grave and something beyond the grave, whatever that might be, for I could not guess what their eyes had seen. They held themselves stiffly, like the dancers of my dream, and their eyes reminded me of the dancers' eyes. But I could not look at their eyes for long, for they held longings and hungers and joys that no living human could endure. I would have touched them in my imperious way, but I knew there would be nothing to feel, for they were ghosts, not vampires nor any living embodiments of death.

In a few moments, they fell silent, and moments after that their images faded and vanished. But it is now past midnight and I cannot sleep, nor can Rose, who lies beside me, because we know something. We are living in a house full of ghosts. We have not seen the last of them. And I don't think we know what they are capable of. Dear God watch over us.

Saturday, 21 December

It has been a hard night and a cold morning. We are all jumpy. My rationality has gone completely, and I look at the world with caution and some loathing. I dreamed of the dancers again, and this time the music that accompanied their slow prancing steps was the beating of drums, staccato blows on stiff leather, and the brushing of their stumps on the beaten earth. They moved in a circle, now sweeping in to touch, now sweeping back to the fullest extent, and someone began to sing without other accompaniment, a low, melancholy song like a *fado*, but I could not make out the words. The dancers kept circling, and as they did so took up the song, though they had no lips to move.

A war is being waged, but we have seen true horror here on the shores of a placid English lake. Bombs fall on London, but true terror lurks between these walls. I would endure the bombing without complaint. But we seem trapped here, at least until there is enough petrol. Dr Raverat may know where I can get some.

One good thing: Octavia's hearing aid arrived by the morning post. I had mentioned it to my parents, and they must have gone at once to order it from a centre that opened recently in Kensington. One part goes round the back of Octavia's ear, and this is attached by a cord to a box containing a battery, which sits in the pocket of her dress. I was inclined at first to leave the whole thing in the box it was delivered in, but Rose thought it might help to distract Octavia, and it has done. Rose has had to go to the doctor's house and then out to visit half a dozen patients. She'll return later if she can. I wish she would make an excuse and get back here straight away. Without her, I have had to experiment with Octavia's aid alone. She says she can hear sounds like banging or bumping, and when I speak she can hear distinct noises. Since she can read my lips pretty well, I have spent the morning with her saying simple words that she recognizes on my lips, so she can start to link these to the sounds she hears in her ears. She has already started to identify several words, and it seems to get easier each time I try. It will be a long road, I can see that, but I am excited about the possibilities this opens up to her, once she has had professional instruction.

Excited and fearful. She has already been hearing things even Rose and I can't hear, and I can't make up my mind whether the hearing aid will increase her ability to hear the dead or make that less likely, by bringing her nearer to the hearing world the rest of us inhabit.

* * *

Rose found an excuse to hand her afternoon visits over to Betty, another nurse. Betty is a newly-arrived trainee with the Civil Nursing Reserve, whom Rose has been training. She's from Keswick, where she spent time with the St John Ambulance Brigade. She can handle the routine visits, with advice from Rose.

We talked again about the situation.

'There is something we need to do,' Rose said.

'One of us,' she went on, 'has to go to the Public Library in Carlisle. We need to know more about this part of Ullswater, more about Hallinhag House, about its history, whether there have been disturbances like this before, whether the names Adam, Clare, Helen and Margaret mean anything and have any connection with the house, alone or taken together.'

'I can do that,' I said, 'provided I can get to the library.'

She took a deep breath. She was sitting on the sofa beside me, and she stretched out her hand and touched mine. Her physicality gave me a sensation of reassurance and prospect after the things I had seen and heard but never felt the night before.

'I think we need to invite Hilary Mathewman back here. In fact, I'm certain we have to do so, and apologize to her for dismissing her opinions so abruptly.'

I opened my mouth to protest, and as quickly closed it. Whatever rationality I had possessed had gone for ever.

'As I said before,' Rose went on, 'she has a good knowledge of local history. Surely you can't have any objection now to seeing her. She got it right about the house. I wish we'd listened to her before.'

I snorted.

'You mean you wish I'd listened to her before.'

'I love you, Dominic Lancaster. That doesn't mean I have to agree with everything you say.'

86

'She may know how to get rid of these creatures,' she went on. 'Or how to persuade them to leave.'

'Persuade them to leave?' I almost exploded.

'Don't tell me you think these things are in any way benign, Dominic. I have never felt such a presence of evil in my life. If I have ever felt something satanic, that's what they are.'

'I just meant . . . that they seem pitiful wretches, just as we thought at first. Poor children, malnourished, badly treated.'

'But they aren't real children, Dominic . . .'

'They are the ghosts of real children. All four of them must have lived at some time, a hundred years or more ago. They may have died from hunger or some sort of mistreatment. If we knew what, it might help us in our search for an answer.'

Mrs Mathewman will be with us this evening at seven o'clock. Rose has explained things to her in full, and she has said it's urgent that we act straight away. She's preparing now, she doesn't say how. The house is quiet, and Octavia says she can't hear anything. She wants me to practise more with her hearing aid, and she seems to have settled down since last night. She's looking forward to Mrs Mathewman's visit.

Later
Hilary Mathewman turned up on time, driving her car, a little Morris Eight tourer, which she says does forty-five miles to each gallon, an important consideration in these days of fuel rationing.

Rose and I went out to meet her, where a rudimentary strip of tarmac runs alongside the lake. Rose slipped her arm round my waist and I bent over to kiss the top of her head with a slightly shaking hand. Against her advice, I had taken some whisky to steady my nerves. As we drew apart, Hilary – as she told me to call her – came up to us, her right hand held out to shake ours.

'Have there been any further manifestations?' she asked.

I shook my head.

'Nothing all day.'

She nodded.

'But you've not gone upstairs?'

'No. It would be hard work for me. I haven't tried to go up there yet. Rose thinks I need to be steadier on my legs before I can tackle stairs.'

'She's quite right. But I wouldn't advise it anyway. Going up there, I mean, dodgy legs quite apart.'

'When I get inside,' she continued, 'I'll go up there again myself. How is Octavia?'

'Her asthma seems much better,' I said.

'No, I didn't mean the asthma. How is she dealing with what she hears and sees in there? It's a lot for a little girl to cope with. And finding her little friend is a ghost, that she has been dead for a very long time.'

'She's frightened,' I said. 'I've tried to reassure her, but she's still frightened. At the same time, she's pining for the little girl called Clare. Clare is the first proper friend Octavia has ever made, and she minds terribly that she can't go about with her, holding hands as they used to.'

'That's understandable,' Hilary commented. 'I would suggest taking her somewhere else for tonight, while we do this thing. But I need her, and I want your permission to have her stay.'

'You mean, the séance?'

She shook her head. In the darkness, I could barely see her.

'I don't do séances,' she said. 'I'm not a medium. If necessary, I'll bring one in. But I want to try this first. What I do is simpler than that. I experience the house and whatever is in it. I have done this about five times before. Then we sit together and try to communicate with whatever haunts this place, and ask it to leave. That may not be easy, but it's worth a try. I suspect the real culprit, the evil thing we've felt, will not turn out to be the children, but if we can push it out it may well take the children with it.'

I frowned.

'Why do you need my permission to have Octavia stay through this?'

'Because she is the focus for what has been happening. Trust me. Whatever is here will still be here if she leaves. But the manifestations only started when she arrived.'

'I arrived at the same time.'

She shook her head. Stars hung down from the night sky, drowning in the waters of a full moon. A barn owl called among the trees, and above it I could hear the clear high cries of a cloud of soprano pipistrelles.

'Whatever these things are, it is not you they want. Not yet. It is Octavia, because in her deafness she alone can hear them. Now, I think it's time we went inside. Octavia shouldn't be left on her own for long at night.'

The door was open. As we went inside, Hilary suddenly stopped, as if listening for something.

'It has started,' she said. 'Let's not waste any time.'

I could detect nothing, either aurally or visually, but Hilary's sense of urgency communicated itself to me. I closed the front door and the three of us walked down the candlelit hallway. We found Octavia where we had left her, at the far end of the dining room, carefully picking through the pieces of her jigsaw. I noticed that she had removed her hearing aid. She looked up and smiled at Hilary. It was a very open, genuinely delighted smile.

'We may as well sit here,' said Hilary, pulling out a chair and sitting at the table. We followed suit.

'Octavia, dear,' she said, twisting round to face my sister, 'why don't you put your jigsaw away? Just the box.'

Octavia nodded and did as she was told.

We settled down. No attempt was made to hold hands. We did not dim the lights, though the oil-lamps we lit here were low when compared with the electrical lighting we had at home, and a light golden glow came from the blazing fire, which had been lit some hours earlier. Our visits in the past had always been in the spring and summer, and for me as a child the candles and hurricane lamps that we lit late in the evening had been an important part of the adventure of coming here.

No one spoke at first. We could hear nothing bar the cold west wind soughing through the trees around us. It sounded chill as it blew flat across the waters of the lake, but its force was broken by the oaks and birches that formed a barrier between the lake and the fell that climbed high above us. To begin with, it seemed as though nothing was happening. I thought that, quite possibly, Hilary Mathewman's presence was sufficient to dispel whatever hauntings there might have been. Octavia sat quietly, and I thought she had possibly fallen asleep. Rose sat close to me and held my hand, not in any promise of a séance, but rather to reassure me. Her breathing was tight, like my own.

Then somewhere far away, but within the house, a thin voice began to sing. None of us could make out the words at first, so thin and soft were they. To begin with, I thought it a single child's voice, as a soloist might sing in a choir. It was a lilting song, and it came towards us slowly. As it approached, I slowly made out other voices, quite how many I could not be sure, all singing low, all singing in perfect harmony, with now one, now another breaking through. The tune was catchy, but unfamiliar.

Then I began to make out some words. Hilary looked at me and whispered.

'It's a children's song,' she said. 'It's called "The Carrion Crow", but it makes little sense. It was popular at the beginning of the last century, in Jane Austen's time.'

Had they died all that time ago? I asked myself.

There was no way of telling where the voices came from. Our candles were burning straight up, the flames like little golden rods. I could hear the words now, as if they were in the room. They sang like children who have been taught the words of a song without understanding it.

A carrion crow sat upon an oak
Fol de rol, de rol, de rol, de ri do
Watching a tailor cutting out his cloak
Sing heigh ho! the carrion crow, Fol de rol, de rol, de rol, de ri do.
Wife, wife! bring me my bow
Fol de rol, de rol, de rol, de ri do,
That I may shoot yon carrion crow
Sing heigh ho! the carrion crow, Fol de rol, de rol, de rol, de ri do.
The tailor he shot and miss'd his mark, Fol de rol, de rol, de rol,
* de ri do*
And shot his own sow quite through the heart
Sing heigh ho! the carrion crow, Fol de rol, de rol, de rol, de ri do.

They appeared at the top of the room, all four of them, their arms intertwined, and I saw at once that the clothes they wore were grave clothes and that they had been in the ground for well over a hundred years. Their song shifted, and now they sang only 'Sing heigh ho! the carrion crow, Fol de rol, de rol, de rol, de ri do'. Their faces were greyish-white and their eyes were pink and their hair fell lank and dirty round their shoulders.

I looked across the table at Hilary Mathewman. Her calm had left her, and she seemed badly frightened. I was frightened enough myself, and another glance confirmed that Octavia and Rose were as rigid with fright as before. I also noticed that a bad smell was filling the room, a smell of decay. It was as if these were not ghosts but actual bodies of the dead translated from their graves, yet they seemed in other respects alive, for they walked and sang as they might have done in life.

And then they began to dance, shod feet clapping against the floor, sticks brought out from nowhere to join in the dance, circling and circling without growing dizzy. I was reminded of the dance in my dreams. They moved in a circle and their faces were wreathed in smiles, but I did not find them harbingers of joy.

At that moment, Octavia said something very low, something I could not make out. It seemed to mean something to the children, though, for no sooner had Octavia spoken it than they started to retreat. The choking smell went with them. They faded into the darkness at the far end of the room, then stood still and fixed their eyes on us, like smoke rising in one place, or shadows converging.

It seemed the greatest possible relief. Had Hilary done something to send them away, or had it been Octavia's short exclamation that had repelled them? It didn't really matter, for this might be the last we would see of them, fading, weakening. Hallinhag House would be fit to live in again.

Or so I thought.

'Hilary,' I asked. 'Is this the end of it? Will they just leave now, go back to wherever they came from?'

'I'm sorry, Dominic, but this is only the beginning. This is not a séance. Let's say it's just a trial of strength. The children don't have anywhere to go to. Hallinhag House is their home. Don't you know that ghosts don't wander far?'

'How can that be? There are no bodies buried here.'

She half smiled and shook her head.

'Have you examined the attic?'

'I didn't know we had one.'

'You do. I have found the attic by looking at the house from outside. It's a matter of finding the entrance.'

I was – and still am – sceptical. I had been upstairs and downstairs many times in my childhood, yet I had never noticed anything of the sort, nor had anybody spoken of one. Since I can't get either down or up for the moment, I prefer to leave any discoveries till later.

Rose turned to Hilary.

'Why did they come here in the first place? To this room? We didn't invite them, did we? What about you, Hilary?'

Hilary pointed at Octavia.

'She is their host,' she whispered. 'Her presence brings them here from time to time.'

As she spoke, I became aware of sounds upstairs. I looked down the room to see the four ghostly children fade and disappear. Without preamble, the room grew bitterly cold despite the log fire burning fiercely in the hearth. Then the fire went out. Moments later, all our lamps and candles were extinguished, as if by a stiff wind, though a profound stillness continued to lie across the room. Octavia cried out as if in physical pain. Rose took my hand and squeezed it tightly. There was another sound from upstairs. Not a footstep. More unformed. It was followed by a repetition of the same sound, this time accompanied by what sounded like a deep moaning. A moment's silence, then a thump and a moan followed by what I can only describe as twittering.

It was Hilary who responded to this first.

'It's coming down the stairs,' she said. 'I don't know what the hell it is, but we should get out of here fast.'

She was frightened. Rose dug her fingernails into my palm. As she did so, I remembered that my cigarette lighter was in my right-hand trouser pocket. I pulled it out and fumbled for the candle that had been sitting on the table next to me. I found it and clicked my lighter. Its flame seemed brilliant in the darkness, and the candle was soon alight as well. With these two flames we lit two of the lamps, then made for the door, Rose constantly with me, holding me safe while I hopped and dragged my right leg. Hilary had Octavia in her arms. We opened the door and made for the hallway. The sound was louder here, and when I looked up the staircase I could make out a shape, large and inhuman, as it thumped and slithered its way down. We got to the front door and got outside. I shut it behind me, as if doing so would create a barrier against whatever was in there. Hilary led us to her car and we piled in, our hearts beating like flags snapping in a high wind. She started the engine just as we saw the front door open slowly, and drove off in a flurry as the opening widened to reveal shadow and something darker than shadow in the doorway.

Sunday, 22 December
Blencathra Cottage
Pooley Bridge

We spent the rest of last night in Hilary Mathewman's cottage, all in one room, all shivering, all sleepless, all in a silence that went on and on, with only occasional interruptions. Hilary drove us there, missing collisions with trees and boulders every few seconds. She used her headlights, swearing at the Germans and whoever made the blackout rules. I expect she'll have a visit from one of the wardens sometime today. There weren't enough beds, but, quite frankly, I don't think any of us could have had the patience to try one, to close their eyes and start to sleep. We're all very tired now, but none of us can rest.

I've decided to find some means to get back to London. First, I have to ring my parents. I won't tell them anything about what has happened, just that I feel trapped at Ullswater and that Octavia misses them. The only phone Hilary knows of is at the Lakeside Inn. Rose will take me there later today, once she and Hilary have had a chance to get things straightened out here. She has offered to put us up for as long as we need, but I don't want to be a burden. All the same, none of us wants to set foot in Hallinhag House again.

Hilary told us that we would have been welcome to stay longer but that she has some visitors coming tomorrow for Christmas. They are old college friends, one she played hockey with on wet, muddy fields, the other an old school friend who had gone up with her in the same year.

Rose took me to the little hotel, the Lakeside Inn, where they have a telephone. I rang my father. He sounded pleased to hear from me at first, and I told him I was getting on well with my leg; but when I suggested coming down he grew angry.

'Don't you realize there's a war going on?' he shouted. 'You of all people should know that. London's being badly hit. They have a new bomb we call Satan, a monster that wipes out everything in its path. Just yesterday our Air Raid Warden told us they have over three thousand unexploded bombs round the city. Your mother and I can get to Russell Square tube in time, once the sirens go off. But you'd never make it in time. You'd be hobbling and mincing along when the first bomb landed on your head. The little shelter we put up in the living room was far too inconvenient, so we gave it to some friends. Don't even think of coming here.'

I said a few words to my mother, wishing her a Happy Christmas. Of course, I said nothing to either of them about the hauntings. They would have visitors, she said, a group of able-bodied young men on leave from the RAF. They wanted to do their bit, she confided.

'There won't be room for you,' she added, 'but once this ghastly bombing is finished, I'm sure we can round up some petrol. Or you might get a seat on a train. You could wear your uniform. That will guarantee a place, that and your leg.'

I told her about the leg and how much Rose had helped me.

'That's absolutely wonderful, darling. You should give her a box of chocolates or something nice for her mother, if she has one. We wouldn't want to see her socially or anything, of course; but it's nice to show your appreciation.'

We talked about Octavia and I explained how well her hearing aid was working. I remained silent on the subject of the voices Octavia could hear. My mother is quite superstitious and would have hysterics if she knew what has been happening.

Of course, without telling my parents that we needed to leave Hallinhag House, and why, I couldn't ask for sufficient funds for a hotel, either. Our dilemma was solved when Rose invited me and Octavia to stay with her and her mother. I leapt at the chance and gave her money to buy whatever is needed for Christmas lunch. One of her patients, a farmer, has given her a splendid turkey, so grateful was he for her attention, and her mother has made stuffing from breadcrumbs and lamb sausage and a Bramley apple pie with fruit from Dr Raverat's garden, where he keeps a fine tree full of apples and songbirds. There is even to be a pudding, made from Rose's great-grandmother's recipe. I wished I could go back to the house to salvage a bottle or two of port, something we had always used in our family recipes.

For all that her mother is well on in years now, I can see where Rose gets her looks from. She's a dainty woman whose features have remained well marked throughout a long life. Her skin has suffered from years of working in kitchens, but she hasn't lost the twinkle in her eye and she has a slim figure any woman of her age might envy.

She has noticed how Rose and I are together, for we make no secret of it. Once, she came in on us while we were holding hands, and I could see she'd taken note of it. I could see she was upset by it, too, but she said nothing and has made no fuss. But how will she be if we announce our engagement, as I hope we will before long? A one-legged man cannot be much of a catch in her eyes, however politely-spoken and well read he may be.

She has started work on a teddy bear for Octavia. His name is to be Bertram, he will have tan-coloured fur, black buttons for eyes and smart trousers of corduroy. Octavia is to be kept in the dark.

I am driven mad by my feelings for Rose. I want her with me all the time, not politely but passionately. I know next to nothing of women, and I believe she is as innocent of men. I love her, and love gives me the most exquisite feelings; but I also lust after her, and it is very hard to be with her, admiring her with great propriety while wanting her bodily. If I'd sailed longer waters and not come to grief as I did, I'm sure that by now I would have sated my curiosity in such matters. Sailors seek out houses of ill repute in every port they enter, and I do not doubt I would have succumbed to the same temptations as my shipmates, even if there would have been better favoured premises for us officers. But I'm glad now that never happened.

One part of me is determined to marry Rose after Christmas, then to return to London with her and Octavia. Or we could marry in London and come back up here to the Lakes.

Rose has a fondness for the little church in Martindale, and that would exclude any sort of society wedding. There wouldn't be much food to go round anyway. Her mother could bake a small wedding cake and we could rent one of the cardboard covers I've heard about, to make it look tall and fully iced outside. There'd be another disincentive for a society bash too, the difficulty many people would face in travelling far with petrol rationing.

Another part of me feels that something must be done first to rectify the situation in Hallinhag House. All we've done so far is run from it. Hilary hasn't been able to do a thing, and I have a feeling she now wants to back off. I have thought of speaking to the vicar at St Peter's in Martindale. It's his province after all. Could he perform an exorcism?

Octavia's role in all this is considerable, for nothing ever happened here until she arrived. I'm worried that, if we don't cleanse the house from the things that inhabit it, Octavia may somehow be trapped. None of this makes any sense, but I would not be surprised to find that the ghosts find her and remain with her.

The house itself is closely bound up with my family, and I'm sure that, once we can establish its history, it may turn out that the ghosts are Lancasters and that the thing on the stairs is linked to the family as well. I have spoken to Hilary about the history of the house, and she tells me Hallinhag Wood was known in the eighteenth century for foreigners. They would come for weeks at a time, and, as far as she could tell, they stayed at Hallinhag House. A name came up frequently: Sir William. Was he an ancestor of mine? I wonder. I'll have to get hold of the family records when I get back to London.

I think we should attend midnight mass in Martindale tomorrow. I may introduce myself to the vicar. If it's still the Reverend

Harris, he won't recognize me. I've changed since I last saw him, and he has never seen Octavia. He's middle-aged, maybe sixty by now, and his wife was a quiet woman who loved Blake's 'Jerusalem' and got the congregation to sing it as often as possible. His sermons were always interesting, filled with quotations from the Romantic poets and references to nature.

Monday, 24 December – Christmas Eve

There was a delivery of post early this morning. Among a last flurry of Christmas cards Rose's packet of photographs arrived, their delivery evidently hastened by the urgency of the season. Mrs Sansom had several cards from old friends, and one from the vicar. There were plenty of cards for Rose, some with robins, most from grateful patients. A couple were from friends who had volunteered to nurse at the front. They were both in North Africa. Their cards were witty: one showed a camel with a robin on his head. The other depicted Santa Claus delivering plum puddings to the German army, each one with a grenade inside. Perhaps that was not much in keeping with the spirit of the season, but none of us would weep if Santa really did make such deliveries. One thing I do know, watching Rose's face as she opened the card (from someone called Pru), was that if she'd been parachuted into German lines, she'd have dusted herself off and set out to find their wounded and succeeded in nursing them back to health.

She and her mother were busy right up to lunch. With so much devoted to tomorrow's feast, stocks of everything are low. But Rose's mother had been given a dozen pullet's eggs fresh this morning – a welcome Christmas present from a nearby chicken farmer for whom she cooked from time to time. She made devilled eggs with plenty of mustard and served them up with leek and onion soup and sautéed salsify with parsley root (we aren't to call it Hamburg root again till after the war). She told us she grew the salsify and parsley root in the back garden. Hitler will never win so long as there are women like Rose and her mother around.

After lunch, Rose's mother went off to take cards and presents to some of the neighbours. Rose was concerned about her going out in the cold and offered to go in her place, but her mother tutted and fussed so much that we let her go, with a strict warning about getting back long before curfew.

When she left, Rose sent Octavia off to play with some of her old toys, and we went to the parlour. Rose made coffee and sat with me on the sofa while we both sipped from teacups. Rose finished her cup and got up to make another. It was instant coffee, but for all that it was very welcome.

When she came back, Rose brought with her the packet of photographs that had arrived that morning.

'They came back quickly,' she said.

'He must have wanted to get everything wound up before the holiday season. And he'll have guessed that some of us might like to see our snaps.'

She found a kitchen knife and opened the packet nimbly yet carefully. I watched her do it with the same neatness I had observed when she cleaned and bandaged my wound.

One by one she put the photographs on the kitchen table. One of *Firefly*, one of me on board, one of herself just before she got on board, taken by myself, several of the shoreline, all blurred by our movement, then some of Howtown. So far, all seemed as it should be. But as I lifted a snap of Dr Raverat's car and turned it over, I found a photograph that soured my stomach.

The photograph showed Octavia as she had been that day, smiling if not grinning. She wore the same frock I remembered her wearing, a light blue coat over a pale green dress. Of course, there was no colour in the photograph, but the contrast looked quite clear in black and white. There was nothing untoward about her, save for that slightly confused look in her eyes. The horror was standing next to her. The girl we had met with Octavia in Howtown was there where she had been when Rose took the snap. But she had changed utterly. She was wearing the ancient grave clothes we saw her appear in with Hilary Mathewman, and her jaw was bound up with a dirty white cloth. Her eyes were closed with pennies and her face had been covered by a thin veil. This veil had come away from the face and lay crumpled beneath the chin, and there were spiders and traces of dusty spider webs. Her face had deteriorated in death, and her shrunken hands were twisted where they fell in front of her. Her mouth was partly open, and some upper teeth protruded. It was the same girl, of that I had little doubt, and her presence next to Octavia sent a shudder across my heart. Rose stared and stared at this apparition.

'Were we talking to a corpse all the time?' she asked.

'Not a corpse,' I said. 'Just a ghost.' The image of her dead body was caught somehow by the camera. She was turning to dust before our eyes. But a moment's thought told me that she had not been dead for very long. It was long to us, but not far from the day of her death, whenever that had been.

We gazed at the image for a while, then I extracted the photograph from the heap and threw it into the kitchen fire. At that moment Octavia wandered in, looking for an apple. We showed her the photographs, and when she rather fearfully asked what had happened to the shot Rose had taken of her and Clare, I explained that it had suffered from over-exposure and the studio

101

hadn't printed it. She just shrugged her shoulders and took a russet to eat outside.

Rose borrowed a four-seater cart with a horse and a farmer's boy to drive it down to Martindale. The little church was packed. I wore my uniform and saw other men and women in theirs, all of us with heavy coats to keep out the cold. There wasn't enough fuel to keep the interior of the church much above freezing. But the tiny choir sang lustily and processed with the priest and his deacon, this latter carrying the processional cross above all our heads.

As it turned out, the Reverend Harris was no longer at St Peter's. He had been called to the role of Navy Chaplain in Barrow-in-Furness, where his wife ran a successful charity shop for the WVS.

His place at St Peter's had been taken by a much younger man, who performed the service impeccably. The church was candlelit and the altar twinkled as if with jewellery set ablaze. Octavia brought her hearing aid, and though she could not make out the words, something of the music got through to her for the first time, and she went through the service entranced. She and I had not yet spoken about the events at Hallinhag House, but she seemed much less perturbed than I had thought she would be.

Afterwards Arthur Cobbit, the sacristan, who remembered me once I introduced myself, told me that the new priest was called Oliver Braithwaite. He was from Durham originally, where he'd studied at Cranmer Hall. I knew nothing of the niceties of theological colleges, and I couldn't elicit from Arthur any hints as to how the Reverend Braithwaite might view an exorcism.

'When you see him later, will you please tell him I need to speak to him most urgently?'

'Can you say what it's about?'

I shook my head.

'I'd rather not,' I said. 'But it's something that won't wait.'

'Well, there's Holy Eucharist tomorrow morning, Mr Lancaster, at eleven o'clock bang on. Would that suit?'

'I'm afraid not. It's a distance from Pooley Bridge to here, with my leg.'

He glanced down as if he hadn't noticed it before, but I knew well that rumour of my condition would have made its way round the district weeks ago.

'I'll tell him, sir, though I can't promise anything, it being Christmas Day and such.'

'Tell him I'll be at Mrs Sansom's, will you? And that it is more important than he can hope to imagine. Tell him, if you like, that there have been disturbances at Hallinhag House.'

This brought Arthur up short. He knew what I meant. His manner changed.

'I see, sir. Yes, he shall want to know about that, sir. I'm glad you've asked him. You could not have asked a better man.'

Despite the cloud hanging over us, Christmas lunch went off exceedingly well. We had a visit from Hilary Mathewman, without her guests, from the village policeman, who is thought to have taken a fancy for Rose's mother some years ago, from some nephews and nieces of Mrs Sansom, cousins of Rose's, who piled in to the cottage unceremoniously. John – Rose's deaf cousin – became instant friends with Octavia, and spent some time helping her with her hearing aid. Their parents arrived about an hour later, sending the children upstairs to play in one of the bedrooms. There were tiny presents for everyone. Rose had even thought to get some for me to give. Mrs Sansom gave Bertram Bear to Octavia, who was wide-eyed and ecstatic. I explained that Mrs Sansom had made him, and Octavia gave her the biggest hug I have ever seen. Not far away, the lake turned to rust and slipped into a dark red that was cut through with streaks of turquoise and jade and amber. The water seemed to sing as the light played on it, as if on the strings of a musical instrument. They have electricity in Pooley Bridge, and our celebrations continued well after sunset.

We had eaten a small tea and were washing up and putting the pots and pans away for the second time that day when there was a knock at the door. Mrs Sansom – who now allowed us to call her Jeanie – answered and found the vicar standing on the step in a flurry of snow. He came in and gave his greetings to everyone, and they felt very privileged to receive a Christmas visit from a man of God in person. They had only ever seen him at a distance before, and there was as yet no consensus in Pooley Bridge as to whether he's a stuffy prelate or a down-to-earth man of the people. From his accent, which I had heard in church, I was inclined to think the latter. It came my turn to shake his hand, and when I did he leaned towards me and said, 'We have to talk.'

The question was, where? This winter has been the coldest in living memory, so I could scarcely ask him to step outside on Christmas Day. But we could hardly talk about the subject facing us while everyone else was still in the cottage.

'I'm not sure where . . .'

He smiled, rather like a child with a new toy, and whispered. 'Come to Dr Raverat's in about five minutes. We'll sort something out then.'

Five minutes later, Rose and I knocked on the doctor's door. It was opened by the vicar.

'Raverat isn't home,' he said. 'He's had to go to visit one of his patients, Harry Niblock, out at Roe Head. I may have to follow him if I can get a lift. He thinks Harry may pass away tonight.'

'Why didn't he ask me to go with him? He won't pass on without trouble,' Rose frowned darkly, furrowing her brow.

The Reverend Braithwaite looked sharply at her.

'Are you Rose the nurse?' he asked.

'Didn't you know? I'm sorry, of course you haven't met me before. I didn't know your name till this morning, when Dominic asked the sacristan.'

Braithwaite smiled his gentle smile again, and I felt a liking for him. Rose broke into a smile too.

'Come in, both of you. Dr Raverat said we could use his study for our little chat.'

It was then he noticed my crutches and Rose's support.

'Oh, I'm sorry, I didn't realize . . .'

'There's no need for a fuss,' I said and walked in. I had made it down an icy pathway without slipping and felt rather pleased with myself.

Raverat had left some coffee on the stove. It was a little stewed, but we were grateful for it all the same.

'Where did the doctor come by this?' I said, holding out a mug for Rose to fill.

'Oh, doctors and priests find ways of getting round the rules and regulations,' he said. 'In the countryside, farmers and old ladies find plenty of work for both of us to do. Now, why don't you tell me what's troubling you? Are you thinking of getting married?'

We both laughed.

'As a matter of fact, we are,' I said, 'but there's time enough for that yet.'

With Rose's help, I told him about my plan for an exorcism. He'd thought the message had been meant ironically. Once he realized I was serious, he lost his good humour and sat opposite me very like a parish priest from the past, regardless of his youth and demeanour. However light-hearted our conversation had been to begin with, in a matter of minutes it took on the darkest overtones. Slowly, it dawned on him that we were telling the truth, or, at least, that we believed what might otherwise have seemed a fantastic tale made up for the Christmas season. He had met Hilary Mathewman and held her in some esteem, and said he would talk to her on the following day.

'But as far as carrying out an exorcism,' he said, 'I'm really not sure how to proceed. The Anglican Church doesn't really do many exorcisms these days. It's seen as rather a medieval affair. Of course, the practice still goes on, and there are those who advocate its return. I can't say that I have an opinion either way. In practice, I would have to get permission from my bishop, and he'd likely send me to Giles Nicholson, who's considered an expert in such matters. Unfortunately, Nicholson's an old man, in his nineties I believe, so this could take some time, and I can see you're eager to get it over and done with soon.'

I had doubted if he would take our story seriously. He's a young man, quite inexperienced in the ways of the world, but I suspect he is something of a modernizer and that this leaves his mind open even to the most bizarre suggestions.

'We'll have to be getting back,' said Rose, 'or Mother will be wondering what's become of us.'

'And I want to speak to Mrs Mathewman, get her opinion about all this,' said the vicar. 'At the same time, I think it would be better if you didn't say a word to anyone else about this matter. The locals are quite superstitious, and that means they can be frightened into anger.'

At the door we shook hands, but just as he was about to turn the key in the lock, he turned to us.

'It has just struck me that there may be another way to do this, certainly a faster one. I'll have to give it some more thought. If you don't mind I'll call at Mrs Sansom's tomorrow about lunchtime. Don't tell your mother, she'll only make a fuss and offer me food. They're very kind, the folk round here, despite their superstitious ways.'

He went on his way. But turning round a few moments later I saw he had stopped yards away, and I saw snow fall on his head and shoulders. All around him, snow drifted down. I could not understand why he was standing still. Then he turned slightly, to face away from Pooley Bridge and along the lake and down to Howtown and so to Hallinhag Wood. And I realized he was praying silently. Despite the cold and the lateness of the hour and the steady washing of the waters of the lake, he stood for minute upon minute, for I do not know how long. In the end he sighed deeply and started to walk to his next port of call.

26 December – Boxing Day

When we got up this morning, Rose asked me outside for a private chat.

'I'm worried that Mother will fuss, seeing the vicar at her door two days in a row. She will think things. With the two of us being together so often and the Reverend Braithwaite on the doorstep, her evil mind will think the worst and decide that we're to be wed, and perhaps the sooner the better.'

I grinned.

'Surely she wouldn't think that.'

'Oh, yes she would, believe you me. So what do we tell her?'

'Tell her the truth.'

'That we've asked for an exorcism?'

'Of course not. Just say we've asked him to call the banns in this parish next Sunday and two Sundays after that. That should be long enough for you to make your mind up.'

She put her hand to her mouth, and I thought she would run off.

'Won't that be pushing things a bit?' she asked.

'How long do you need?'

'For what?'

I took her hand.

'To tell me you love me. To agree to marry me. Or to tell me to go back to London.'

'I will marry you,' she said. 'There's nothing I want more. But until this business with the house is done with, I don't see what we can do. Even if the exorcism works, I don't want us to move in there as a couple, to start our married life in a house with such associations. You may have to move back to London and live with your parents. I have to stay here to keep my job. With the war on, we might have to stay apart again for years.'

'You're forgetting one thing. Neither of us will be called up for war service. I may not have made it clear, but my family is quite rich. Things are tighter because of the war, but our money in this country is substantial and well managed. Once we're married, we'll move back to London and rent a small apartment. And we'll find you a nursing job down there, if you think you'll need one. Now, what is it? Banns or exorcism?'

For some moments, I thought she would storm off, but to

my utter surprise she stepped up close to me and put her arms round me.

'I don't know what I'll do with Mother,' she said, 'but she'll find a way; she always does. What about Octavia? Will she go back to your parents?'

'You're sure about this? You'll be my wife? I mean, we hardly know one another.'

She smiled.

'We know one another well enough. I feel as if I've always known you.'

'Yes,' I said, 'that's exactly how I feel.'

'Well, then, we don't have any choice. When I was younger, I had lots of boys. It was kissing and holding hands, but it was childish enough, it meant nothing. In the end, I might have married one of them, but I knew I didn't want to. This thing I feel for you is an adult thing. When I kiss you, it won't be a peck on the cheek. I want to be naked with you, I want to make love to you, I want to be part of you, and if I have to marry you to get all that, I'll walk down any aisle in the kingdom. But first we have other matters to discuss with the minister.'

We had just finished lunch when Reverend Braithwaite knocked at the door. Rose's mother made a fuss. He had come through something not far short of a blizzard on foot, and was covered in snow from top to bottom, even though he hadn't come very far. We put him in front of the fire and Octavia took his hat and scarf. He looked intensely at her, remembering no doubt what we had told him of her involvement in the hauntings. Moments later she returned with a plate of Christmas cake, while my future mother-in-law (though she didn't know it yet) brought a pot of piping hot tea for us all. Grace, a twelve-year-old cousin, brought the cups and saucers, giggled and went beetroot, then dashed back through the door. Heaven knows what Jeanie was filling their heads with in the next room.

When all was settled, we squeezed together, Rose and I, on the hard wooden settle and the Reverend Braithwaite on a rocking chair on which he moved backwards and forwards gently while he talked.

'I have been giving your problem a lot of thought. I also spoke to Mrs Mathewman, who corroborated your story and also impressed on me the need for urgency . . . And I may have the answer to your predicament,' he said. 'In many ways, it suits me better than having to seek permission from my bishop, something I don't think he'll give, especially not to someone as young as myself.'

I sipped my tea, hot but without sugar or milk.

'If you're old enough to be a vicar, surely . . .'

He shook his head. I noticed he was wearing a pullover over his dog collar. I wondered if he had a wife and whether the vicarage he lived in was decent. Some parishes are quite poor.

'And what is your answer?' Rose asked.

'Ah, the answer. Well, I can only surmise, but it may work. I am a good friend of Declan Carbery. He's an Irishman and the Catholic priest at Ambleside. I've consulted him on various matters in the past. Catholics have a better understanding of exorcism and related matters. I think he may be able to advise us or even do something directly. Would you approve of that?'

We looked at one another. Rose nodded, and I followed suit.

'Good, that's settled. I'll get in touch with him later today. He's a good man, you won't have anything to worry about.'

Just as he was about to go back out into the snow, I stopped him.

'Reverend Braithwaite. I have another favour to ask of you. Would you . . . would you read the banns for Rose and myself

110

in church this Sunday? I don't know if I have to pay anything, but . . .'

'Well,' he beamed, 'I got it right first time, didn't I? I can always spot a couple in love. Congratulations. The banns have to be read three times, a month apart. But you'd be surprised how many couples are getting hitched with this war on.'

Once he was gone, we invited Jeanie into the little parlour in order to tell her our news. She almost leapt out of her seat, then sat there, her face wreathed in smiles.

'You've been dark horses, both of you. You won't know this, sir, but ever since she first set eyes on you, it's been Mr Lancaster this and Mr Lancaster that, then Dominic this and Dominic that, and I shouldn't wonder if it's Darling this and Dearest that by now.'

Rose blushed, having done her level best to keep her feelings from me for as long as possible.

'Mum,' she said, and I thought it very quaint that she used such a term of endearment, for I did not doubt that my mother would never have allowed me to take a similar liberty with her. But my mother is a cold woman and a fit help-meet for my father, who is a cold and ungenerous man, above all to his family. They would be told of the forthcoming nuptials at the last moment. Why should they complain when there's a war on and everybody now gets married *à la mode*?

Friday, 27 December

We saw some evacuees today, a bunch of little boys and girls who came out to the Lakes about a month ago from Liverpool. Their homes have been badly hit, and it's likely some of them will have nowhere to go back to when the war is finally at an end. We spoke to their teachers, who had brought them in from various farmhouses to see Dr Raverat. Rose had spent the morning with them, doing basic check-ups, while the others were taken in to see the doctor. They're all from the slums, and Raverat reckons they'll go back to Liverpool plumper and healthier than when they left. The free milk ration alone, he thinks, will build better bones and teeth.

'Why don't we take them all for a sail on the lake?' Rose asked.

'There's an awful lot of them,' I said. 'The *Firefly* will only hold one passenger at a time. I'd need a bigger boat.'

'What about one of the steamers?'

I nodded.

'Not a bad start. I doubt if any of the children have been on the water in any form. Though there's a ferry at Liverpool, isn't there?'

Rose nodded.

'Well, we could do a trip on the steamers, I suppose,' she said. 'But having been out on the *Firefly* . . .'

I agreed.

'There are some larger yachts for hire. And the club has a selection of life jackets, including some for children. How many children are there?'

'Seven.'

'That makes eight with Octavia. Let's look into it.'

There was just time to get down to the club. Raverat was happy to lend us his car, once he knew what we planned.

'You should come too,' I said.

He shook his head and smiled uneasily.

'Never could stand water,' he said. 'Not like you types.'

'You mean us one-legged misfits?'

He snorted.

'I mean nothing of the sort. I mean you daredevil types, out there shooting, driving sports cars, and yachting from here to San Francisco. I'm an ordinary man. I can't stand sports, the thought of flying scares me witless, and I can neither swim nor go on the water in any way.'

'So you won't be coming with us?'

'I'll wave you off at the dock or whatever you call it. And I'll see if I can rustle up some grub for your little wards.'

'Shall we say tomorrow?' I asked.

He thought for a moment.

'Yes, why not?'

Rose had a list of all the families with whom the evacuees lived, and we drove round to tell them of the arrangements for tomorrow, causing much excitement. We hoped the weather would turn out all right. It would be cold, and there might be a stiff breeze, but that would give the boat speed, which the children might enjoy. The next port of call was Bluebell Cottage, where Adrian Humphreys lives. Adrian is the Secretary of the yacht club and an old friend of my family. I used to see a lot of him in the days I came here as a youngster. He helped teach me to sail, in fact I reckon I learned more from him than anyone. He had never been a professional sailor or served in the Navy, but he'd sailed a lot at sea, in the Irish Sea and out in the Mediterranean.

I explained our plan for the evacuees and he listened in sympathy. At first he didn't like the idea of kids from the city clambering over one of our yachts, pulling on the sheets, chucking the compass overboard, and cutting the anchor loose. I talked him down from that. Rose and I would be in charge, and any high jinks would bring an end to the outing. That would mean the kids would police themselves.

He said we could use the *Kingfisher*, a thirty-two-foot yacht with a cabin where the children could sit round a long table to eat.

'She's really a bit long for the lake,' he said, 'so we're thinking of towing her to the coast, if it's safe to do so. I won't ask for a hiring fee. I'm sure those children could do with a day out on the lake.'

'I don't think they've had a day out of any description.'

'Really? Well, I'm very sad to hear it. All the more reason, then. Yes, indeed, all the more reason. I'll crew for you too if you like. Now, do tell me how your parents are . . .'

Later

The Reverend Braithwaite turned up late this evening, accompanied by a much older man, whom he introduced as the same Father Declan Carbery he'd mentioned earlier. Carbery is the Catholic priest from Mater Amabilis in Ambleside. He's Irish, but has been here for over twenty years, a priest in an area that has very few Catholics.

We made him welcome and Rose's long-suffering mother helped her daughter bring tea and biscuits she had baked earlier that day. She was surprised to see Father Carbery, for she had never set eyes on a Catholic priest in her life before, and had never imagined she'd be inviting one in for tea. There's a certain amount of prejudice about Catholics in these parts, something that has its roots in the large numbers of Irish men and women who came to the region in the last century. There were Catholics and Protestants among them, and they brought their old prejudices with them on the boats that brought them from Ulster.

I quickly came to like Father Carbery. He must be in his seventies, but he's as bright as a button and untroubled – so far as I can see – by physical infirmities. In his clerical garb, he looked as though he had been a priest from childhood. I can imagine him having been born with a dog collar, dressed in a black suit. His face is wrinkled and his eyes have a depth and sadness no young man could have. But his smile is curative. I think his parishioners must love him, and I am sure those who receive the last rites from him must go more easily on their long journey.

After the Reverend Braithwaite made the introductions, we sat down and talked. To be more precise, Father Carbery talked.

'I had a visit from Oliver Braithwaite yesterday. He told me all you had told him about events at your house. Hallinhag House, is that correct?'

I nodded.

'Very good. Now, I would like one of you to repeat to me what you remember, what you have seen, what you have heard.'

I told him what I could, and Rose corrected me a couple of times. He listened impassively and said nothing until I had come to a finish.

'Thank you, Dominic. That is all very helpful. Your account tallies almost exactly with that of the good reverend here. Now, he has told me that you asked him if he could perform an exorcism in your house. Is that correct?'

We both nodded.

'And he has, I am sure, explained to you the difficulties he faces in doing this from within his church. He does not rule it out, but he foresees difficulties in bringing in their nearest expert in this field, a field in which the Reverend Braithwaite has no experience at all. Now, it was his conclusion that he might instruct me to perform the exorcism for you in his place. I take it you would have been agreeable to this proposal? That you harbour no negative feelings about Catholics? I would ask you to be honest about such feelings, if you do have them.'

I had no idea what Rose felt on the subject, but what she said summed up for us both.

'Father,' she said, 'if what you do get rid of the things in the house, then I don't care if you're a witch doctor from the depths of Africa.'

'Very good. I can see you're both in agreement on that score. But here is what I have to say. Thinking this through, I cannot see my way to performing an exorcism, nor will I approach my bishop, nor will I recommend that the Reverend Braithwaite go to his. An exorcism is not appropriate to this situation, and I think it could make things worse.'

'But surely,' I said, 'the house is possessed in some way. Surely there is something there that has to be exorcised.'

'Mr Lancaster, you must let me be the judge of that. I do not believe there is anything in the nature of demonic possession. There appear to be some children who haunt the building. Four of them have been seen outside the house, and one was standing next to your sister, Octavia.'

'She seemed very real at the time. The little girl, I mean. Her name was Clare.'

The priest nodded.

'Yes, ghosts can often seem as real as the living. Not for very long, of course, but for a while. Let me tell you what I propose. I will go with you to the house tonight. I will go inside alone, and I will try to speak to the children and persuade them to go.'

'What about the other thing?' Rose asked. 'The thing we heard coming down the stairs?'

Father Carbery shook his head.

'You have never actually seen anything on the stairs, and I don't believe there was necessarily anything there. We must focus our energies on those poor children, who have been only too visible.'

116

He hesitated for a second, then got to his feet.

'Since it has been a long way from Ambleside, I'd like to get this over with before it gets too late. Are you in agreement?'

We looked at one another. I could see that Rose had misgivings, but she nodded.

We sent Octavia to bed, but I think she guessed what we were up to. She took my hand tightly and wrote something on my palm that I could barely understand. 'Don't go inside' and 'Look after Rose'. Rose came up behind me and kissed her on the forehead. The car was waiting for us outside.

Later

Coming to Hallinhag House late at night and in the dark, we saw that a full moon lay nailed to a sky of stars, bright points of freezing light that held the silver disc in its orbit. The house faced us, lightless, like an enormous shadow that had come out of the end of things to be here, to entice us inside. Not one of us wanted to be there. I argued again with the priest, but he spoke to me calmly and with authority. He was the expert, and I could not deny him.

Wrapped in blankets, the three of us stayed in the car. Rose's mother had prepared hot flasks with soup and tea, and we drank to keep our spirits up. We'd been supplied with hot water bottles, and though Jeanie must have guessed something was up, she never once enquired. Father Carbery went inside alone. The door was still open, as I had left it. He closed it behind him, and the last thing we saw was the light of his torch. It is hard to know what he saw, if anything, as he entered. I cannot believe he was not frightened.

'It's such a lovely house, I've noticed it before. Dominic, your family is very fortunate to own a place like this,' said the Reverend Braithwaite, 'but, to be honest, I'm not unhappy we haven't gone in. The very thought of phantoms makes me shake, it's such an unnatural thing. I would hate to go in there and see or hear anything uncanny.'

'There may be nothing tonight,' I said.

'What makes you think that?'

'Octavia isn't inside. All this started when she appeared. She was never in the house before, on account of her asthma. I can remember many happy years in the house, and there are no family stories that I know of that talk about strange appearances.'

We talked like this for a while, then distracted ourselves with stories of the sea and the local parish. Rose remained quiet, even when we asked her for her nursing tales.

I don't know how much time passed. Half an hour? An hour? It felt more like two, and it was very cold. Our hot water bottles had long ago lost the least trace of heat. Fresh snow had started to come down and was drifting over the windscreen. An owl, shivering in its nest somewhere, cried out against the cold, and moments later I heard a robin call from a lakeside tree. It brought back memories of the night-birds who sang outside my window, the corncrake whose rasping calls kept us all awake into the early hours.

Frustrated by such a passage of time and no activity that I could see, I made up my mind.

'I'm going in,' I said. 'Something has happened, and I don't think it's something good.'

Oliver Braithwaite turned in his seat and looked back at me.

'I won't let you go alone. This is my parish, you are my parishioner, and this is a spiritual matter.'

'Me too,' said Rose. If I touched her, I could feel her shiver from the cold. 'You need someone to help you stay steady on those crutches.'

'Then come to the door with me,' I said, 'but don't come in.

If I call, then join me inside. But I don't think we should all pile in together.'

Thinking it over after we got home, it seemed to me that Rose's offer had made her love for me clearer than any number of declarations of simple attachment would have done. I know how much she loathed the very thought of returning to the house, yet there she was, defying her own fears to go in with me.

When we reached the door, I noticed straight away that all was silent inside. Rose and Oliver Braithwaite protested again that I should not go inside without them, but they quickly saw that I was adamant in the matter.

'The first sign of anything being wrong,' I said, 'and I'll be out of here faster than you can guess.'

'Darling, you're hardly nimble on your feet. What if you trip and fall, what if you're knocked out? We wouldn't hear a thing. You've got five minutes to look round, then we'll go in, regardless of what you say.'

I weighed this up, then nodded. My brain was screaming to get far away, to get all of us out of there. But I pushed the door fully open and stepped into the hall. Oliver Braithwaite had made me a curious little device, using a band of elastic to hold my torch on my head, so that I could use both hands for my crutches. I was glad for the light, but the moment I entered I knew something was wrong, something I had not anticipated. As the beam of torchlight played across the stairs and walls, I had to think twice. It looked as though I had stepped into a different house. Everywhere, wallpaper had fallen away in strips and rotted. The carpet beneath my feet felt spongy, and when I looked down I could see that it too had rotted and had developed holes in places.

Father Carbery had said he would head for the dining room, since that was where the children had been seen before. But

119

when I went there, I could see no sign of him. I went to the living room, the kitchen and several other rooms on the ground floor. He was in none of them. My heart sank, realizing that he must have gone upstairs. It was the only possibility. But what else waited for me upstairs, if I went up there?

I left my crutches against the wall at the bottom of the staircase. I could smell the rottenness, as if something had died. Using the banister to hold me upright, I slowly began to climb. I could hear nothing, but as I neared the top, I saw something flicker past my line of vision. Something silent. I thought about Octavia, and the idea that she focused the voices of the children and made them audible.

I looked up and saw four children, standing on the landing above: Adam, Helen, Margaret and Clare. They held dolls in their hands, dolls with blackened faces holding sticks, and they moved the dolls to and they moved the dolls fro, and the dolls danced, and when they touched the sticks together the children laughed. The children, like lords of this house of the dead.

'Father Carbery?' I called. I ignored the children. The priest did not answer. I was deeply troubled, seriously worried about the old man. I should not have agreed to let him come here alone. We should have stood up to him and gone in with him, as I had originally planned.

I reached the top of the stairs, fearing one of the treads might give way. But none did.

'Father Carbery? It's Dominic Lancaster. Are you up here?'

There was no answer. Nor was there any other sound. But when I looked along the corridor that straddled the upper floor, my torch picked out something. One of the children was standing there, the boy, the pallor of his skin intensified by strips of moonlight that fell through a side window. Moments later, the other children appeared beside him.

120

'Father Carbery?!' I yelled. Then the children moved to one side and I saw him, prostrate and crumpled, like a man who has fallen from a great height.

I went straight to him. Bending down was hard for me, but I managed it. I put my hand to his neck. He was freezing cold and there was no pulse.

At that moment, two things happened. Rose's voice called out for me from downstairs and a man's voice said something I could not at first understand. Then I did understand it, he was telling me to take the priest and go, never to return, to leave the house and the children here where they belong, to lock the door and never come back.

I shouted down to Rose and Oliver Braithwaite and told them to come up to help me take Father Carbery away, since it was not something I could do on my own.

While they manhandled the priest's body, I got down holding fast to the banister. At the bottom, I found my crutches. Above, I heard a sneering laugh, and when I looked up I saw him, a man in what looked to be the clothes of an eighteenth-century aristocrat.

Then another man's voice came from above. I looked up and saw, half-way along the staircase, a second man in eighteenth-century clothes.

'You heard the man. You're no longer welcome in my house. Leave now and don't come back again.'

How we got the priest through the door I hardly know. I had the key this time, and I locked the door, as though it would make any difference. We had to put the dead man sitting upright in the front seat. Oliver Braithwaite drove. He seemed very shaken by whatever he'd seen when he went up the stairs.

'Where do we go with him?' I asked. 'Do we have to get to the hospital?'

Rose said we should just drive to Dr Raverat's and ask him to examine the body. After that, no one said a thing. The car hummed through the night. I could still smell that fetid odour, that rotting smell. As we got near Pooley Bridge, Rose turned to me.

'What did the first man say?' she asked. 'Could either of you make out what he said?'

I knew the answer. None of the others would have known.

' "Get out," he said. "Never come back." Something like that.'

'But what language?' she demanded. 'It wasn't English, I'm sure of it.'

I nodded.

'No, it wasn't English,' I said. 'It was Portuguese.'

Saturday, 28 December

Raverat had turned a light Bedford van into an ambulance. It was still pretty much a van, and would not have been suitable for any badly injured patient, but it turned out to be perfect for transporting a dead body. He drove off at first light to take Father Carbery's body down to the morgue at North Lonsdale in Barrow. That was this morning, and we don't expect him back till tomorrow. They'll perform a post-mortem, and he'll report back to us when he returns. I've no idea what they'll find, but I'm confident they'll put it down to old age. Whether something frightened him to death, whether he'd taken himself out of his depth spiritually and mentally, we'll never know. I doubt very much they'll find anything of an overtly physical nature. The Reverend Braithwaite says he'll give a heavily doctored account to Carbery's bishop and hope no questions are asked. Braithwaite himself is badly shaken. He's at home now.

When we got back last night, Octavia was still waiting up for us, although Rose's mother had gone to bed a couple of hours earlier. My little sister looked tired, but it was clear to me that she had been unable to sleep until she knew all was well. I had decided to tell her nothing about Father Carbery's death. We persuaded her to go to bed, which she did reluctantly.

Jeanie had left out a flask of hot milk, a small bottle of brandy and some honey. We made milk toddies in a pair of mugs adorned with drawings of cats, and we drank them without speaking. That made me feel a lot better, I can tell you.

As I put my empty mug down, I smacked my lips and turned to Rose.

'Rose, I've decided to marry your mother instead.'

'That may be a good decision. And if I marry your father, I can become a lady of leisure. '

I shook my head.

'Don't even joke about it. You won't like him and he won't like you.'

'I don't have to like him. But if I marry him, I'll be quite rich, and if you marry my mother, you'll be well looked after. I warn you, though, that you'll be better off with me in bed. I've never been in bed with a man before, but I'm a nurse and I know what's what and what goes where. On the other hand, if you marry me, my mother comes as well, so you'll get a double bargain, a mother-in-law to make you toddies and a wife to take you to bed.'

We joked a little like this, using humour as a means of winding down. I could not get certain sounds and images out of my head.

'What did you mean?' asked Rose. 'When you said he spoke

in Portuguese? Surely that isn't possible. There have never been any Portuguese here.'

'I'm not so sure,' I said. 'Certainly, dozens of Portuguese businessmen and their wives visited Hallinhag House and toured the Lakes during the summers since this place was built.'

'What did he say?'

'As far as I can remember, it went much like this. "*Leve o padre a cabo, vai embora, e não volte nunca mais. Eu, Senhor Guilherne e os crianças ficaremos em casa. Pertencemos aqui. Em esta casa. Finalmente, feche a entrada a chave.*" It means, "Take the priest and go away, and never come back. The children, Sir William and I will stay in the house. We belong here. In this house. Finally, lock the door behind you." '

'You understand all that?'

'Rose, my love, my family has been doing business in Portugal for about three hundred years. When I was growing up, my father brought in a succession of tutors to teach me Portuguese, and I used to get practice when we visited. I'm fairly fluent, though I really have little use for the language now.'

'Perhaps you will again,' she said, 'when the war is over and you can go there. Your father will need someone to take over the business when he's gone.'

'He'd never let me. He'd as soon have an outsider as his own son.'

She looked tenderly at me.

'We shall see,' she said.

We did not go to bed, but sat in our chairs all night, for we were afraid, each of us, of being alone. '*Leve o padre a cabo . . .*' went through my head while I lay awake, and when dreams came at last, I saw the dancers capering again. Before they had had no faces, now they had no heads, and they capered madly, their legs kicking high in the air and their arms flailing as if it were St Vitus's Dance. Sometimes they would bend and pick up their heads and replace them on their necks, and the eyes would open, and look out glaring at the world.

We were woken by Jeanie coming down about six o'clock. She said nothing about finding us there, and set about warming the little kitchen and making breakfast. Rose went up and fetched Octavia. She had not slept well either, and told me she had seen the children, that they had seemed ill, that their staring eyes had been eaten up with grief or mourning or suffering – she could not say which.

'They are changing,' she said. 'Their eyes are not the same, their bodies are not the same, their clothes are not the same. They have scars on their faces, something is wrong with their skin.'

And when I thought back to the night before, I had to agree that she was right. The children had changed in perceptible ways. And the skin on their cheeks seemed darker and thicker than previously.

We sat down to a fine breakfast of bacon and eggs. Jeanie kept a couple of pigs in her back garden, in a little hut of corrugated iron, and when the inspectors came they knew better than to examine that part of her property. This was the countryside, and keeping pigs was common practice. Of course, she always feared the arrival of a new inspector come up from Liverpool or some other city, an inspector who would take the trouble to go outside, an inspector who would confiscate her precious pigs and fine her heavily.

The Reverend Braithwaite arrived not long after we had finished. He looked very glum as he came in, but bucked up tremendously when he was offered a plate of bacon and eggs and the single sausage still lurking in the meat safe. These were the perks of vicarhood. He sat down and ate while we watched. At least he still had a good appetite, but he looked poorly. Talking of ghosts in the abstract, as he had done, was clearly one thing, but seeing them in reality, hearing the men's voices at the end, finding dead a man who had been alive not so long ago – all this had taken it out of him.

When Jeanie started on her chores, she asked Octavia to help. The two of them got on very well together, and I had hopes that they would see a lot of one another in coming years. Rose, the vicar and I retired to the living room.

Braithwaite told us he had spent the night in prayer. He looked as though he had gone without sleep for hours.

'I can't deal with this,' he said. 'There was such a sense of evil in the house, and when I found Declan Carbery lying dead . . . I will have to go to my bishop in Carlisle, perhaps speak with the priest who handles exorcisms. I feel completely out of my depth.' He stopped to compose himself, and after a moment continued, 'Perhaps there's some rational explanation for all this. I don't mean the hauntings as such, but something historical. They are the ghosts of real children, perhaps children who once lived in the house.'

'Of that I'm quite sure,' I said. 'There are the two men as well. One is Portuguese, but the other could well be an ancestor of mine, if he owns the house. That means he has a direct connection with my family, and the children too perhaps. If there's something in the family records, maybe we can use it to get to the bottom of the thing. Perhaps there's something they want and can't do for themselves but want us to do for them. Do you think that's possible?'

'The children, yes,' said Rose. 'I think they're quite innocent in this, but they seem to be trapped by something. And speaking of them, have you forgotten your promise to the evacuee children here? The trip on the lake? I thought you'd made arrangements.'

I sat back. The trip had gone completely out of my mind.

To be honest, I really wasn't in the mood for an outing, but I didn't like to break a promise to any child, especially these children. Their hosts were going to scrimp with their ration books to put together a picnic that would be just enough for seven healthy kids. After all that, I couldn't very well back out.

Afterwards, Rose and I both wished we had.

Later

The *Kingfisher* was a lovely boat, with twin sails and a leather-upholstered cabin down below. The deck had been polished to perfection, the sails were pure white with purple stripes, and the rails looked safe enough for the children.

Adrian helped us pick them up one by one. Their pallid faces were shining with anticipation. I think they had never before gone anywhere or seen anything outside their own dark, narrow streets, where they would have been sitting targets for Hitler and his bombs if they hadn't been evacuated. They had arrived in clothes too thin to keep the cold out, and I think they had suffered badly from this unusually freezing winter. I couldn't have taken them on the water today if they'd still been dressed in their old clothes, but their hosts had been using their ingenuity. They'd heard that the WVS runs a Centre in Barrow, where they take in old things, fix them up, and sell them on to make money for the organization. There's a woman called Nella Last who's in charge of all this, and she and her helpers do incredible things with clothes. A couple of the host women had taken the bus there before Christmas and had come home with more pullovers and overcoats than they could manage. People had helped them on board the bus home, the conductor didn't charge them a halfpenny more, and there were willing hands to get their purchases off the bus in Pooley Bridge.

So our little rabble weren't shivering, and the fresh air seemed to be putting a glow in their cheeks. I had an uncomfortable feeling that none of them would want to go back home to Liverpool when the war was over. I wrapped Octavia well in her little red coat and Rose found a beret for her that she herself had worn at about her age. It was black and went well with the coat. As I put it on, I noticed that Octavia had what looked like a rash on her jaw. I asked Rose to examine it and she said it could be eczema or early signs of acne. She would ask Dr Raverat to look at it when he got back.

My spirits were lifted by the trip. I tried as hard as I could to put last night behind me. When we ferried the last two children to the landing stage, they were jumping up and down in delight. Some of them had already made friends; others had been isolated on their farms, but didn't take long to start chatting.

We spent some time instructing our landlubbers about how to behave on board a yacht. They were issued with their life jackets. On questioning, none of them said they could swim, so I insisted they keep the jackets on all the time. A cold wind blew past and the surface of the lake grew a little choppy. I decided that a strong following wind would help speed things up and make the sailing part of the trip more exciting.

And so it was. We set off, Adrian at the helm, myself on the sails, while Rose brought up a couple of kids at a time on to the deck. Some of them started out frightened, the movement of the yacht quite unlike anything they'd ever known on trams or buses. Most of them settled quickly and got the hang of how it all worked, and those who didn't retired below decks.

Cherry Holm is a tiny island near the end of the lake, with Glenridding to the west and Patterdale to the south. It has a single tree that I, in my urban ignorance, take for an alder, and masses of bushes. There isn't much room to sit and contemplate the universe. Not much room to run and play. On the other hand, I'd thought, perhaps it was just as well that they wouldn't be able to scarper off in all directions, getting lost and getting into trouble.

It's not far from the shore at Glenridding to Cherry Holm. There was no hope of mooring the *Kingfisher* at the island, but we dropped anchor on the lakeside where Glenridding comes down to meet the water. Adrian manoeuvred the dinghy round to the side, and we lowered the children down, first a group of three, then another of three, and finally two. Then he got Rose down and came up to tie a line round my waist so he could lower me into Rose's waiting arms. Then he took us over to the island, to a spot where there was a wooden dock with a cleat to tie the dinghy up. The kids were bubbling over with enthusiasm.

I was churning inside, for my thoughts were with Father Carbery and how he must have died. I hoped it had been quick, but feared that it had not. Would Dr Raverat have the answer when he came home today? I hoped to hear that it had been a heart attack, something without mystery.

But my worries prevented me from thinking about Cherry Holm Island and the children I had brought there. Dear God, if only I had used my head, a great tragedy might have been averted.

Later

I have had to take a break from writing, to steady my nerves before recalling the rest of our trip to Cherry Holm. When I was younger, as I have mentioned previously, I often repaired there alone or with friends to play or read. It was a benign place, big enough in a child's eyes to serve as a kingdom. My father never came with me, for which I felt some relief. He did talk to me about brave and honourable men who built shining realms by standing up against all others and beating them to submission. He tried to instil this idea into me, and to show me how a well-run business was a ruthless enterprise, that a true businessman was as much a warrior as any general, that such a man should be cold-hearted, pitiless, single-minded and self-interested.

The kingdom I built in my imagination during my childhood days on Cherry Holm was built on kindness. At home or at Hallinhag, my father frequently boasted of how he'd sacked this or that worker, or even one long-serving member of his board. He had a reputation for hardness, and prided himself in the fact that his workers all lived in fear of him. From an early age, I resolved to be unlike him and swore that if, by some twist of fate, I should ever become head of the firm, I would cancel his petty rules and regulations and institute a new regime based on loyalty and trust. And I would deal with my customers in the same way.

It was dreams like these that I took with me to Cherry Holm back then, and today I set foot there with equally naïve thoughts about giving my abandoned children their first real chance in life. Hallinhag House and its ghostly inhabitants faded in my mind and were blown away by the light breeze and the cries of laughter and excitement from the children.

Rose in particular knew how to deal with them. She would sit down with three or four at a time and take out their lunches, chatting with them while she distributed the food and saw that everybody got their fair share. She was everybody's favourite that day, and the more I watched her with the children the more I loved her and wanted children of our own. Much to her credit, she spent what time she could with Octavia, who was having her usual difficulty in winning acceptance from the other children, children with little notion of politeness, experienced in the rough ways of the school of hard knocks and unfamiliar with the deaf.

The lunches came with bottles of pop, most of it ginger beer, and we quickly learned that several of the children had never tasted such luxury. There was much hilarity when the first one burped audibly. Apart from Octavia, there were four girls and three boys, and I determined, once there was a chance, to talk to them in order to find out what sort of lives they had lived until now. They had seen some bombing, but didn't like to speak of it. If I asked, they said they weren't afraid of Herr Hitler, but I could sense that, underneath, they took the bombs very seriously indeed. They had seen houses brought down on top of whole families, bodies laid out among the ruins, children running through the streets in search of their fathers and mothers.

After lunch, we decided to play hide and seek, a game they were all familiar with, but which they had only ever played in the street. There wasn't much space on Cherry Holm, but it offered some very enticing bushes, quite a few good-sized rocks, and the sheer excitement of being outside amidst such stunning scenery. Off behind Glenridding, the children could see the great height of Helvellyn, one of our country's highest peaks, and everywhere they looked were the tallest fells and the most wooded slopes. There was snow on the higher parts. I thought it could not have been a better place for them to play.

Then we did another countdown, and Rose and Adrian and I dutifully closed our eyes. Then, half-way through, I heard a low cry and opened my eyes. Some of the children were running to the east side of the island, as though in alarm. Octavia was standing right next to me, and from her expression I could see that something was wrong. She gestured, but I could not make out at first what it was about. Rose and Adrian still had their eyes covered.

Just then I noticed someone moving on the western side, where the island faces Glenridding. The late afternoon light was dipping towards the west, but it still had some time to go, and it shed a grey beam across the lake and on to the island, near where the dinghy bobbed at the landing dock. Someone was walking towards the little jetty. Four children. Three girls and one boy. But even as I watched, three of the children turned and looked at me. I knew them, for I had seen them before, and they turned their heads and continued to walk with young Jimmy Ashton just behind, as though transfixed. I called out, bringing Rose and Adrian to the alert, and I pointed.

'What is it, love?' Rose asked.

'Can't you see them? The children from the house.'

Adrian strolled over from his place near the tree.

'Is something wrong?'

I pointed towards the jetty, where the four children stood while Jimmy climbed on to the narrow deck. Jimmy must have taken off his life jacket earlier, and it was suddenly clear what was about to happen. I shouted at Jimmy and started clumsily off in his direction. He did not behave as though he had seen me. Next thing I saw, the four ghost children had vanished and Jimmy was in the water.

Adrian saw it. I could not have got there in time, and I couldn't have swum in any case, but he hared off to help. Rose turned to me.

'I saw them just before Jimmy fell in. You should stay here. I don't want you to have an accident. Adrian will get Jimmy, but I have to see to the children. I want them all together, in case the other children return.'

It made sense. I told her to get them together, but to bring them to me, so we could deal with them in a united fashion. In our concern for them, I almost forgot Adrian's more urgent mission at the water's edge. But it was not long before we got the youngsters in one place, all shivering, some weeping, and it was a little after that when Adrian turned up, dripping wet – for he had gone into the freezing water. He had dived and dived repeatedly, but the water was murky and the boy had gone in deep and could only be found now by a professional diver.

'What happened to Jimmy, miss?' asked one of the girls.

'He fell into the water,' Rose replied. 'I think he tripped or something. Did you see what happened?'

'Yes, miss. We all saw it, didn't we?'

Heads bobbed up and down.

'There was four children a bit older than us. They must have come across on a boat, 'cause they wasn't here when we got here. They appeared out of nowhere and spoke to Jimmy, then somebody said they was ghosts and we all scarpered.'

'It was me thought they was ghosts. They was wearing real old clothes and their faces was like dead 'uns. I saw my old man when he was dead, and they looked just like that. That's why I said they looked like ghosts.'

It has been a very hard day. The evacuees are terrified still, and there will have to be an investigation into Jimmy's death. Rose has been in tears since it happened and won't leave my side or Octavia's. Her mother only knows that one of the ragamuffins from Liverpool has suffered a terrible, unnecessary accident. She says little, but there is an unspoken accusation that a yacht trip to Cherry Holm – at the far end of the lake – had been an indulgence too many. We didn't argue, but we passed the whole thing off as an accident owing to the boy's over-enthusiasm in a world he knew too little of.

133

Adrian had seen the four children as well, and had taken them for evacuees, dressed perhaps in old rags they had brought with them. But as Jimmy fell from the planking, the children seemed to vanish, and he could not work out where they had gone to. We told him. We told him their names, Clare, Adam, Helen and Margaret. Ordinary names, names for ordinary children. Names for the living and the dead.

After supper, there was a knock on the door. Rose answered and brought in two visitors, the Reverend Braithwaite and Dr Raverat, both men looking the worse for wear. By this time, Jeanie had smelled several rats. Rose tells me that her mother got her alone in the kitchen and confronted her with it all.

'Don't tell me this has aught to do with you and your supposed wedding to Mr Fancy Man Lancaster. I don't believe you're getting married, though I could well believe you're with child and that's what the good doctor is doing here. Shame on you for making such a fool of me. Shame on both of you.'

An argument followed, audible in part to the rest of us. I tried to get Octavia to go upstairs to bed, but she shook her head violently. She had something quite different in mind.

'We'll have to tell her,' I said. 'This isn't fair on her or Rose.'

The others nodded in agreement, so the Reverend Braithwaite went to the kitchen and asked them to come out. They did so reluctantly, but the presence of the minister and the doctor did much to calm Jeanie down. We all found seats. Rose came over and sat on my knee, putting her weight more on my sound leg than the other.

Oliver Braithwaite spoke first.

'Mrs Sansom, I owe you an apology, in fact we all owe you one. We've not been straight with you, and that has roused your suspicions when there need not have been one. First of all, you need to know that Rose is carrying nobody's child. The doctor here will confirm that.'

'Actually,' Dr Raverat said, 'I think that's a matter between Rose and her fiancé, but I'm certainly unaware of any pregnancy.'

'The thing is, Jeanie,' the priest went on, 'something bad happened today, something related to earlier events. To things that happened down at Hallinhag House.'

And so he told her. Not in too much detail, but as fully as made sense. She was a credulous woman and had no difficulty taking the supernatural stories on board. The one thing that caused her real distress was his full account of today's tragedy. As he was telling it, I remembered the story of her husband's death, lost in the lake when trying to save a boy who had fallen overboard. She seemed to see an echo as well, and when I looked there were tears on her cheek.

'Have they found him?' she asked. 'The little boy.'

The doctor nodded.

'We got a couple of divers in from Barrow,' he said. 'There's a navy vessel due to go out the day after tomorrow, so all the crew were ashore to put things shipshape before they set sail. The divers went in with underwater torches and found the lad at around eighty feet. They attached a line and brought him up with a winch. He's at my surgery for the night, and I fear I'll have another journey to Barrow tomorrow morning.'

We talked a little longer and managed to get Jeanie back to her old self, as much as was possible under the circumstances. The Reverend Braithwaite spent some time alone with her.

We told Octavia it was time for her to go to bed, but she shook her head and reminded Rose that she planned to ask Dr Raverat about her rash.

'Surely you can see the doctor during his regular surgery,' I said. 'He's not very far away.'

There was a flailing of arms indicating a measure of agitation on Octavia's part.

'It's okay,' said the doctor, 'I'm here now. Why don't I just take a quick look?'

He took her to a back room, where Jeanie kept oddments for her sundry activities. Five minutes later, he came back, smiling and patting Octavia on the back.

'Nothing to worry about,' he said. 'Now, run up to bed while the rest of us have a chat about your brother's wedding.'

She waved goodnight to us all and headed for the stairs, exhausted by the day she had just spent.

When she had gone, Dr Raverat did not sit down, despite the temptation of a glass of ginger ale and brandy that had been left on the mantelpiece for him. He took me to one side while Rose and the minister chatted.

'Dominic,' he said, 'I'm not in a position to comment on Octavia's rash at this stage, but I must warn you that I don't like the look of it. It's not eczema, it's not acne, it's not dermatitis, it's not psoriasis – in fact, it's nothing I've ever seen in my surgery. I'd like her to be looked at in hospital on Monday, just for a short visit. The North Lonsdale in Barrow has a good skin unit, and there's a first-class man there, Robert Thackery.'

'She'll be alarmed if we say she has to be seen, after you've given her the all clear.'

'I'll think of something. But I don't like the look of the lesions, and I'd rather get her there sooner than later. I'd like to enlist Rose's help in this. Skin conditions can get out of hand if you don't nip them in the bud. Now, if you don't mind, we have another matter to look into.'

He took his brandy and ginger ale and gulped it down in a single mouthful. The others had grown quiet. He sat down.

'This has been a stressful day,' he said, 'more for you folks than for me, although I've not been free from worry. I went to Barrow late this morning and was in time to catch Philip Woodroofe when he came out of the post-mortem. He's released Father Carbery's body for burial and written "not known" for the cause of death. It was the best he could do. He brought me in to the post-mortem room and showed me what he'd found. I have never seen anything like it, and I've attended quite a few post-mortems in my time. I still don't believe what I saw. Somehow or other, the priest's body had been drained of blood. There were traces of powder in the veins, and when this was tested it turned out to be dried blood. But it wasn't all the blood from the corpse, there were only a few teaspoons of it. Philip and I agreed that making this more widely known would serve no purpose. I'm only telling you now because you were involved in his death.'

'What about the little boy?' I asked. 'The one they took to the North Lonsdale today. Does there have to be a post-mortem in his case? I'm afraid they may find something similar in his body, and that would open up questions I'd rather not see asked.'

'I can understand your reservations,' Raverat said, 'but I'm afraid there's nothing I can do to prevent it. The police are already involved, and you must know how the wheels start to turn once official forms are filled and everything takes its course.'

We parted in a melancholy fashion, and the moon took its light away behind a grey and windblown cloud. It grew colder than it had been. Rose came to the room where I slept with Octavia.

'I wish I could stay in bed with you,' she said. 'You need cuddles and goodness knows what.'

I held her close.

'It's not cuddles I need. It's what I want but can't have.'

137

'I'll get into bed with you, if you really need me to.'

I shook my head, though she couldn't see me in the darkness.

'I think it would give Octavia a fright, and if your mother got to know of it, we'd never live it down.'

'You wouldn't have time,' she said, 'for she'd kill you first.'

'And what about you, Miss Sansom?'

She tweaked my ears.

'She'd lock me up in the pigsty and never let me out again. You wouldn't want your desperate passions to lead me to that. I wouldn't even be able to visit your grave. Think of that: you'd be a lonely corpse.'

At the mention of corpses, she stopped talking.

Our mood quickly grew solemn.

'What about the children?' I asked.

'The evacuees?'

'No, the others,' I said. 'The dead children.'

'What about them?'

'Are they lonely, do you think? They have that look about them. They seem abandoned. It's in their eyes. Some of the evacuees have a similar look.'

'Yes, I thought that.'

'But why are they lonely?' I asked. 'The ones at Hallinhag, I mean.'

'Dominic, perhaps it's a similar loneliness. The evacuees have been torn away from home. Perhaps these children don't really belong in Hallinhag. Perhaps they come from far away.'

'From Portugal?'

'Maybe.'

She drew away. Octavia was stirring, as though our speech disturbed her. I still had to write this diary sitting on the side of the bed, using a small lamp. Rose and I kissed, and the kiss made the longing we had just joked about something very real and very troubling. She got to her feet and left. As she got to the door, she turned.

'We have to look into that possibility,' she said. I nodded and she left.

There was nothing much we could do today. Rose, her mother and I went to St Paul's Church in Pooley Bridge, where the vicar said special prayers for little Jimmy Ashton. His friends had been brought to the church by their hosts, and they sat in the front pews, and were addressed each by name by the vicar, in his sermon. They were white-faced. I smiled at them as they came in, but they turned their faces away, as though holding me responsible for the tragedy. I knew I could not tell them who the four children were who had taken Jimmy away from his friends and enticed him on to the landing stage. Oliver Braithwaite had said nothing to his colleague about the ghastly event at Hallinhag House. The vicar of St Paul's was an elderly man, very set in his ways, who regarded tales of ghosts and demons with withering scorn.

After morning service, the Reverend Braithwaite laid on lunch at the rectory over at Martindale for Rose, myself and Dr Raverat. The doctor was a pious man in his way, though not a regular churchgoer, but he drove us over so we could talk it all over again. We came up with no better answers. I had a particular worry, that if the four dead children were free to walk so far beyond Hallinhag House, then there was no knowing where they might turn up next, or what child they might not seize on and hurry to his or her death. We knew of no way to

139

stop this happening, other than to keep the evacuees in sight at every moment. But it was unlikely that even Dr Raverat's say-so would carry the necessary weight. The children still did not have a school to attend.

It was Oliver Braithwaite who came up with a solution to that problem. Plans had already been laid for a couple of teachers to come to Pooley Bridge from Keswick. The little town was host to over one thousand schoolchildren who had been evacuated there some time ago. Pupils from the working-class schools of the North East rubbed shoulders with girls from Roedean and Newcastle High. Our little group should have gone there too.

'There's nothing to be done about moving them to Keswick, not at the moment anyhow,' said the Reverend Braithwaite. 'The schools administration has become very muddled up. The Board of Education hasn't handled the evacuations particularly well. But there may be a ray of light. St Katherine's College is a Liverpool institution for student teachers. It has decamped in its entirety, and is now snug and happy in the Queen's Hotel. I'm thinking that one or, at the most, two teachers from Liverpool would serve our young men and women very well. What do you think? While you are all in Barrow tomorrow, I can ring and put in a request for this and ask for someone to be sent by Tuesday at the latest. I know Hilda Brayfield. She's a local councillor who lives over on Chestnut Hill. She's one of these people who serves on every committee that's going. We're both on the local education committee, where I'm the Grand Panjandrum for the church schools. If I get her ear, it should be stamped and signed by tomorrow afternoon. Pooley Bridge church hall should prove a very satisfactory place for a school.'

I held up a hand.

'Oliver, will you ask him if he has a deaf teacher to spare? I don't think Octavia should be left out of this.'

'Now you mention her,' said Raverat, 'I'd like to have another look at that rash.'

When lunch was over, Dr Raverat, Rose and I returned to Pooley Bridge and Rose's cottage and the doctor went upstairs to find Octavia. We heard his voice briefly, then there was silence. I made a pot of tea for Rose, Jeanie and myself, and we settled down and switched on the radio. The lull in bombing over Christmas was still in force, as though commands had been given, as though Hitler and his minions respected Christmas and ate strudel and stollen and washed it down with glasses of Kirschwasser, singing 'Silent Night', and embodying love for all mankind before sending their planes out again to strafe and bomb and swallow the world. I fear we are in the lull before some storm.

Jeanie said nothing more about the hauntings at Hallinhag House nor the death of little Jimmy Ashton, though I think he, in particular, was in all our minds. We had sung 'Jerusalem' in the church that morning, and Jeanie said it was her favourite hymn. Rose smiled and said neither this nor that.

Dr Raverat knocked and came in. I thought his face looked rather grave.

'I'm sorry to take up more of your time,' he said. 'But I won't take long. I have to visit a dying woman a couple of miles from here, and I may be there all night. Unless, that is, Rose – would you be willing to come with me?'

'Where to?' she asked.

'Out at Inglewood. She's an old retainer, and the family never let her go, even after she was too old to do any work. I don't think there'll be much nursing involved, but I'd find you a help. I'm a bit down since yesterday, and tonight isn't likely to spread good cheer.'

Rose handed him a cup of tea.

141

'There's not much sugar, I'm afraid,' she said. 'We have to wait till Wednesday before we can get more.'

'This is fine.'

He looked at me.

'Dominic, I'm growing more concerned about Octavia. Her rash has grown since I last saw her. That's highly unusual, indeed I can't think of a single skin condition where the rash grows so quickly. All the more reason for her to see the consultant tomorrow. If things go as I expect this evening, I'll get Rose back by midnight and I'll pick you all up first thing.'

He drained his tea – it's bad form these days to leave anything in your cup or on your plate – and we all shook hands and saw him to the door.

Later

Rose is back. Octavia is fast asleep. I am writing a little extra for today. I turned on the radio just a few minutes ago and came in on a BBC news broadcast, the midnight news. Bill Pickles, a Yorkshireman whose voice it is usually a pleasure to listen to, brought bad news from London. The nation is still taking it in. Tonight, there was a massive raid on the oldest parts of London, an attack so fierce it caught the firewatchers out. The result is a firestorm in which some of the capital's oldest and finest buildings, including at least a dozen churches, have been gutted. St Paul's was attacked by incendiary bombs, and Mr Pickles says it was only the tireless work of the firewatchers there that prevented the whole cathedral going up in flames. I don't know if Bloomsbury has been targeted, but the bombing is still going on and is expected to continue all through the night.

I have looked at Octavia while she sleeps and, although I do not have Dr Raverat's expert eye, I can see that something is

142

wrong. She isn't right in herself. This business with the house has depleted her, and from some things she has conveyed to me, she holds herself responsible for it all. I have asked her why she thinks this is, but all she has suggested is that the children would not be able to speak if it weren't for her. She thinks they use her, that they use her deafness as a means to communicate. I see her suffer more and more each day, and I want to get her away from here, from Hallinhag House back to London.

Monday, 30 December

We drove to Barrow this morning, and all our conversation was about the raid on London last night. As the adult Londoner among us, I tried to describe to the others the layout of things, where the City lay in respect to landmarks like Buckingham Palace or the British Museum, which is five minutes from where my family lives. Octavia practised with her hearing aid. Rose had made a list of words on paper, and she would show one at a time to Octavia while repeating the word, then asking me to do the same. She had borrowed some magazines from the surgery, mostly *Good Housekeeping* and recent issues of *Life*, which were sent from the United States through London. The most recent copy to reach us, from early December, showed Ginger Rogers on the cover. *Good Housekeeping* was full of illustrations and advertisements that showed household items Octavia was familiar with.

At the hospital, I stayed in the waiting room while Rose accompanied Octavia inside. Dr Raverat headed for the morgue. I read some of the *Life* magazines. Some time passed, fifteen or twenty minutes, then the door opened and Rose asked me to come in. She did not smile as she did so.

I was introduced to Dr Thackery. He was a thin man of about forty, with half-moon glasses and a stethoscope round his neck. He seemed friendly enough, but grave.

'I would like to ask your sister some more questions. Nurse Sansom knows some sign language, but it's not adequate. I believe you are better positioned to carry out that task.'

I nodded. He took me to one side.

'Very well. But before we do that, I have to tell you what I think is wrong with Octavia. When I was younger I worked at the Naini Asylum in Allahabad. I worked with its founder, an American called Sam Higginbottom. Of English ancestry. He knew Gandhi very well.

'Now, you may think from its name that Naini is an asylum for the insane. It is not. Naini was set up to treat and care for lepers. When Higginbottom set it up, they were treating the condition with chaulmoogra oil, now they use a drug called Dapsone. I have treated hundreds of lepers, and I have no hesitation in saying that Octavia has somehow contracted the disease.'

'But that's impossible,' I said, 'there is no leprosy in this country.'

'I'm afraid that's not entirely correct. It's extremely rare, but there are perhaps just under one hundred new cases a year. Many are patients who have come here from abroad, from countries where the condition is more prevalent. Take my word for it, Octavia has contracted leprosy. And it seems like a quick-acting variety. I've taken swabs from her rash. I want to test them against leucoderma or vitiligo and one or two other conditions, but I know my tests will come out in favour of leprosy.'

Rose came over and took my hand.

'There is treatment,' the doctor said. 'Remember too that leprosy, despite the myth, isn't particularly contagious. It may be very hard to find out where and how she was infected. Do you know if she has been abroad recently?'

'Not at all,' I said. 'She'd never even been to the Lake District before this trip.'

'All the same, I'd like her to see a friend of mine at the Hospital for Tropical Diseases. They've moved from Gordon Street out to the old Dreadnought Hospital in Greenwich, on account of the Blitz. What a terrible thing that was last night. I'm glad we have such brave lads to go up and fight them off, but it's monstrous all the same. I'm told you have a house in London. Is it safe?'

'As far as I know.'

'Glad to hear it. Where is it?'

'Bloomsbury.'

'Will there be any difficulty in getting Octavia to the hospital?'

'I doubt it. We have a car, though that's not to say we can get petrol. The Underground doesn't go to Greenwich, otherwise that might have been the most efficient. We could always take the tube to the nearest station and have a cab take us the rest of the way.'

'Good. You may get an extra petrol ration to cover any hospital visits she may have. The man you need to see is called Raymond Martin. He's a Belfastman, from Queen's University originally, but if anyone can understand what's wrong with Octavia, how she came to be infected, and what the prognosis may be, he's your best bet. I wouldn't lose any time in getting her to him.'

'I was already thinking of going back down to London. It's a case of getting tickets.'

'Don't worry. I'll see to that. We have ways of obtaining things for medical purposes. You can pay me when you get back.'

As we were leaving, I turned back to the doctor.

'Tell me, doctor, is there any history of leprosy in Portugal?'

145

He looked at me quizzically.

'Why do you want to know?'

'My family has close contacts with the country.'

'Has Octavia visited the country?'

I shook my head.

'Not yet, no. But we often have Portuguese visitors.'

'I see. Well, the answer to your question is yes. Just this year, they've started work on a very large complex to accommodate and treat leprosy patients. It's to be called Rovisco Pais, just outside the university town of Coimbra. They've invited me over, but I can't possibly see my way to travelling on the Atlantic while hostilities continue. They expect large numbers of patients. As you may know, it's still quite a backward country, and levels of hygiene aren't what they should be. So, yes, it's possible.'

Wednesday, 1 January 1941
Bedford Square, London

A new year today, but little cause for new hope. It seems incredible that we're back again and that Rose is here with us. She's in the guise of my nurse and helpmeet to Octavia, and that's how she'll stay until things settle down. The journey took nearly nine hours, with delays at every step. Of course, we had to change trains a number of times, and everywhere we went there were soldiers and airmen and sailors grabbing any vacant space, all carrying kitbags and most of them making a dreadful racket. Rose wore her uniform and sorted them out with cries of 'Disabled sailor and child!'. I had to wear my uniform too: I'd been advised to take it up to the Lakes, and today I was grateful for having done so. A lieutenant with half a leg flushed the worst of them out. A very polite RAF captain made a sort of barrier to keep the riffraff away and stuck to us like glue all the way to London. He flies Spitfires somewhere on the coast – nobody can ever say where they are based, of course – but he was coming back from leave after visiting his wife in Windermere. He'd only had time for a day with his parents, who live in Keswick. We'd left at seven in the morning, for I wanted to be safely in London – if 'safely' is the right word – well before curfew, but it was already dark when we pulled in at Euston. The car was waiting for us, of course, although my parents didn't deign to meet us, and we made it home just in time.

It didn't take long to understand how bad the Blitz has become. Bombs were dropping for hour after hour, and I urged everyone else to head for Russell Square tube, but they weren't having it. My parents had never liked being underground with the hoi polloi. So we sat in the flat, listening to that implacable sound of German bombers growling overhead and the ack-ack batteries like great doors slamming right above us, and the whistling of bombs followed by the crump of explosions that always sounded as if they were next door.

It was a short raid, but frightening.

'I don't know how you can live through it all,' I said. 'It's absolutely terrifying. Nurse Sansom,' I continued, 'don't you think so?'

'I've never been through anything like it in my life.'

'What exactly do you do for my son?' asked my father. I could see he was building to one of his moods, and I hoped he wouldn't turn on Rose. She squared up to him.

'I keep an eye on his wound, cleaning it every day, and I make sure he takes his painkillers. Of course, I see to Octavia as well now.'

'Surely any old skivvy could wash the man's leg,' he pursued.

147

'Can't see what use a regular nurse would be. Of course, you're a pretty little thing. No doubt he's proposed to you already, the way he's always doing with the women. I'd go back to your hospital and keep well clear of him.'

'Father,' I butted in, hoping to steer him off. 'We have to speak about Octavia. It's one of the reasons Nurse Sansom came down with me. It's for Octavia that we returned.'

'What's wrong with her? She has her hearing aid now.'

Octavia sat to one side, unable to read our lips. My mother faced her, silent. She had not hugged her daughter or spoken more than half a dozen words to her.

'The GP at Pooley Bridge has recommended she be taught by a special teacher for a year or two. The hearing aid, which we got on Nurse Sansom's recommendation, is helping. But to make it a success she needs someone who has worked with children wearing such aids. However, that's not what we have to speak about.'

In unemotive language I explained about the rash and the diagnosis given by Dr Thackery, followed by his referral of Octavia to the Hospital for Tropical Diseases.

'Stuff and nonsense!' exclaimed my father when he had heard me out. He got out of his chair and stood right in front of me.

'People in this country don't get leprosy,' he bellowed. 'It just doesn't happen. She's never been to one of those filthy places like India, there's no way she can have acquired it in London or the Lakes. You're wasting all our time with these horror stories. Don't you think we have enough trouble here with Jerry dropping his bombs on our heads without you bleating about some quack doctor in a godforsaken hole like Barrow-in-Furness who's been filling your heads with balderdash about leprosy. No doubt he charged you a fancy fee.'

I had to stand. He was towering over me, and it was hard for me to find an easy way to get to my feet. Well, my foot. Rose saw at once what I was trying to do and came across and took one elbow, lifting me so I now stood face to face with him. Then she stepped aside.

'So the cripple can stand,' he crowed. 'So long as he has a little woman to drag him up.'

'Damn you,' I said, 'you're damned offensive. I was wounded fighting in the war. You're a bully and unchivalrous, and I have had enough of it. I will take Octavia to the hospital in Greenwich and we will have a definitive answer from this man Martin. You are many things, Father, but an expert in tropical diseases is not one of them. And don't throw the Blitz in our faces. If you had the least idea what's been going on at Hallinhag House, you might think that what you've been through here has been pretty mild.'

I thought he blanched. Did he know more about the house than I'd suspected? Or was he just not used to me standing up to him. What would be his reaction if I told him the truth?

'I think it's time you were in bed, Mr Lancaster,' said Rose, coming closer and taking my arm.

'Be sure he doesn't invite you into it.' This was my mother, and these were almost the only words she'd spoken that evening. I was tired, but I had lost my patience.

'If you must know,' I snapped, 'I have proposed to Rose and she has done me the honour of accepting me. The banns were read in Martindale parish church on Sunday. We would like to have your blessing.'

My mother sniggered. My father looked disgusted.

'We will talk about this another time, Dominic. But I will say here that my blessing will not be forthcoming, nor, I am sure, will your mother give hers.'

There was a snort at my mother's end, and a shaking of her head.

'I am sorry this has discommoded you both so much,' I said, holding back my real feelings with great difficulty. 'My nurse has suggested it's time for me to go to bed, and I will take her advice. She will see me into bed and then go to her room. When we marry, it will be a different matter, as you will see.'

'I would not be so casual in using the word "when". You may not marry. I may not permit it.' My father was enjoying this. Rather than encourage him, I took my stick from Rose – I had switched to it from my crutches thinking, foolishly, I would impress my parents with my progress – and she helped me through the door.

Later

Rose and I took Octavia to bed. She had followed us to the door and gone upstairs behind us. Our apartment is large and extends across two floors. My parents sleep in separate rooms on the lower level, near the reception rooms and the kitchen. They had made no allowances for my condition previously, and now I still had to climb the stairs to my room above, this time with Rose's help.

Octavia asked why Father and I had argued, and I told her that it was just because I'd announced my engagement to Rose. Still, it took some time to settle her down. The air raid had rattled her. Some of the blasts had been loud enough for her to hear, and she had been aware of everyone else flinching every time a bomb exploded near at hand. She told me the steady growl of the planes was still playing through her brain.

We got her into bed and found Boris, the teddy bear she had left behind, his red button eye still intact. Octavia introduced him to Bertram and told us they were already friends. I knew my parents would never call in to wish her goodnight. Once Octavia was convinced that there would be no further raids that night – though none of us knew that for sure – I made to put out the light. But as I did so, she shook her head violently and asked me to leave it on.

Rose asked if she would be able to sleep with the light on.

'Maybe,' Octavia answered. 'I don't know. But I've done it before.'

'Yes, but that was in Hallinhag House because of the things that are there.'

'I know,' Octavia said, 'but something has followed us from there. We're not alone.'

We asked her what she meant, but she just shook her head. Her eyes began to grow heavy, then closed, and before very long she fell asleep.

My parents had gone to their own beds by then too. I heard their doors close. The housekeeper, Mrs Mayberry, came up to ask if we would need her any longer, and we said no, we'd go to our rooms now that Octavia had settled. Mrs Mayberry kissed Octavia goodnight, and I remembered her many small kindnesses when I was a boy and later, and how thoughtful she had always been to Octavia. Without her, Octavia might never have known anything but the cold formalities of life in this palace of an ice king and queen.

Mrs Mayberry went back downstairs and I heard her go to her room. Rose found my stick and gave it to me, then helped me quietly out of the room. She took me along the corridor to my room and we went inside. I got to the bed and sat on it, then I noticed that Rose had turned round and was busy locking the door.

'Rose? What are you doing? Surely you aren't frightened that . . . ?'

She put her finger to her lips and pulled the key from the door.

'You should tell me to leave,' she said, 'or ask me to stay. If

151

I stay, I will get into bed with you. The way your father spoke to you earlier, and his boasting that he might stop us marrying have made me rethink things. And the bombs that fell tonight have startled me. They will fall wherever they will fall, and perhaps we'll die and perhaps your parents and Octavia and Mrs Mayberry will die. None of us can trust to life any more. I think that if I died tomorrow and became like those poor children in Hallinhag House, I would go through eternity regretting that we had never known one another in the flesh. I may be no more than a nurse and I may not aspire to join your elevated family, but my body is a woman's body and you have a right to see it and touch it, just as I have a right to touch yours.'

And she touched the top button of her blouse, and her fingers moved in a slow dance across the other buttons, unbuttoning until the blouse came away and she stripped it from her arms. I sat on the bed and watched and she removed her brassiere and she stood facing me bare-breasted, taking my breath away. If I had felt any hesitation about what we were doing, it fell away from my heart in those moments. I had never seen a woman's naked breasts before, though I had seen them in paintings in the National Gallery; yet the moment she bared them for me, I couldn't help but feel an overwhelming desire to look at them and touch them.

Then she removed the rest of her clothing. She did it without drama, not as an exhibitionist might undress, but daintily, with a nurse's efficiency, I suppose, yet at every step inviting my gaze, and I watched what I had never watched before, and when she was naked, it was almost more than I could bear, and my need to touch her was overwhelming. She turned off the overhead light, leaving my little bedside lamp to shed some light on our lovemaking.

She smiled, but said nothing as she came to me. It took her

not much more than a minute to unfasten my shirt and trousers and to remove my underwear. For some reason I felt self-conscious of my amputated leg, even though Rose had bathed and cleaned it every day since I first met her.

'This will be better if I get on top,' she said. 'We can practise later with you in the same position.'

I didn't care which way up either of us was. She kneeled over me, angling her body so I could explore her with my hands. Then she lay against me and used her hand to help me enter her. As I did so, I began to stroke her back and arms and buttocks. I continue stroking her gently, but with growing force, and as I did so her skin changed under my hands. It started by becoming very slightly rough, like fine sand, and in my ignorance I thought this was the normal state of a woman's skin in love-making. My brain was no longer working well. I was stranded between pleasure and delirium, but I moved my hands across her like someone who's been doing the same thing every day for forty years. I wanted to follow every curve of her, but the more I did so, the rougher her skin became, and then I woke up. I was running my hands over what felt like the cold scales of a fish or a snake. And where she had been caressing me, suddenly I felt something like sharp claws. I looked at her and pulled her head back and saw red eyes glaring down at me. I screamed and pushed her away from me, off the bed, and I pulled myself away to the other side. My stick was a fine ramshorn specimen that Rose had bought in Pooley Bridge for me, and I stretched out and got hold of it, ready to fight off whatever had taken Rose's place.

I looked down at where she had fallen, and all I saw was Rose's naked back. I saw no sign of scales, of a monstrous fish or a venomous snake. She was curled up on the floor and sobbing bitterly, and I didn't know just what I had done to her.

153

'Rose,' I said, but she did not respond. 'Rose, we have to speak.' She still refused to speak to me, and she got to her feet and started to put on her clothes again. All the while, she did not cast a single look at me. I realized that there was no point in trying to engage her in conversation, no point in trying to explain, if I could explain. Our romance was over, our wedding would never take place.

Thursday, 2 January

The second day of the new year. Winter and the war are still with us, and my ghosts are still with me, more vividly than ever. Because of last night's manifestation, I have lost everything, and my restless spirit cannot find peace. Rose and I took Octavia to see Dr Martin this morning. She – I mean Rose – does not speak to me, and I dare not speak to her, even though I want to explain to her what really happened. I cannot tell Octavia what has happened, it would be impossible to explain to a child. There was a note for me from Rose this morning on the breakfast table. She writes that once she sees Octavia settled here, she will take the first train north. I am more devastated than I can say, yet I have no one to whom I can talk. My parents are like walls without doors or windows, no one I know well, no friends, are still in London, and Rose's mother is the last person I could make my confidante. Perhaps the Reverend Braithwaite will listen, or maybe Dr Raverat. But they are far away. Embarrassment on top of misery, then, misery on top of fear.

When we got to the hospital, it was buzzing with voices and the sound of feet running on linoleum. Soldiers are coming home from the Western Desert with strange illnesses and the armed forces want them out of London and back to the front within days. Others are left behind as I was, to recover more slowly or to die. A good few soldiers visit the Berka, the red light district in Cairo, and are shipped home with a mixture of venereal diseases and other horrors endemic to Egypt, like hepatitis, schistosomiasis, typhoid or West Nile fever. God, I wish they could ship me out there, where the sands could swallow me alive and erect a monument to my folly.

Rose went in to see Dr Martin alone, posing as Octavia's nurse. I was left to sit in a bleak waiting room, a room empty of anyone but myself. This was a temporary home for the hospital. There were no magazines to read, no one offered me a cup of tea. Nurses and doctors of all sorts passed by along the corridor next to me. Voices echoed beyond, sisters shouting orders, trolleys humming past, nurses laughing and growing silent. I tried to think about what had happened. I remembered what Octavia had said not long before it all happened: '. . . something has followed us from there. We're not alone.' It was the only thing that made sense. Not the children, surely. But that other thing, that unnameable presence, had it been capable of implanting falsehoods in my brain? Or the Portuguese man or the man called Sir William – had it been their doing?

Time passed. I looked at my watch from time to time, as though I was keeping watch on board ship. An hour went by.

A nurse appeared, dressed in the Queen Alexandra's Nursing Service uniform, familiar to me from my days on board the *Aba*. I noticed she was wearing a ribbon, blue vertical stripes on a red background.

'Is that the new George Medal?' I asked, while she helped me to my feet.

'I've been abroad,' she said. 'I can't say where, of course. We had a lot of fighting. Well, that's it really.'

155

I reckoned she couldn't be more than twenty-five. Whatever she'd done to earn that medal, it hadn't been insignificant.

She took me to the consulting room, where the doctor, Octavia and Rose were waiting for me. Rose didn't look in my direction as I came in or when I was helped by the nurse onto a chair. The doctor shook my hand.

'Lieutenant,' he said. 'You're doing very well for an injury of that sort. Isn't he, Nurse Abrahams?' His Irish accent was immediately noticeable.

'He must have had excellent help.' She smiled. Her with her medal, me with my artificial leg, all trophies of the war.

'I had the best help imaginable,' I said.

The doctor asked Nurse Abrahams to take Octavia to a nearby room, and when they had gone he turned back to me.

'Lieutenant Lancaster, I asked Rachel Abrahams to take Octavia out, because I don't think she's ready yet to hear the news I have to give you. I want to confirm Dr Thackery's diagnosis. Octavia certainly has leprosy, and it seems unusually aggressive. He measured her rash when he saw her. The rash has grown noticeably since then, and it is getting thicker and raised above the skin. My conclusion is that Octavia has tuberculoid leprosy, which is the least damaging form. But I have gone over every part of her. I have seen a number of circular patches which are likely to be the formation of new outbreaks. That is not such good news, in fact they give me cause for concern.

'You must think very hard about how your sister might have contracted the disease. It really isn't easy, you know. I believe you think she may have been in contact with some people from Portugal. Can you find out if any of them had leprosy? If they were business contacts of your father, he may know if they had.'

156

He gave advice and handed me a month's supply of Dapsone, a medicine most hospitals would not have had to hand.

'She needs to come back to me once a month. You can make an appointment for February when you're leaving. Nurse Abrahams will show you where to go.'

'I noticed she has a George Medal.'

'Yes, indeed. We're very proud of her. She came here straight from the front line. She doesn't talk about it much, but as I understand it she saved a dozen men from under heavy fire. The First Aid unit she was with was smashed to pieces. Most of her chums were killed. She has relatives in Germany, but they've all disappeared and been taken to camps. All Jews, of course. Nobody knows what will happen to them. But if I can manage it, I won't let her be sent to the front again. She's done her bit in my opinion. Just as you have, young man.'

All this time, Rose kept herself turned away from me and said nothing. When I left, she let me go first, coming quite a few paces behind. Nurse Abrahams found us and fetched Octavia. She took us to the entrance, where our car was waiting for us. I got into the rear with Octavia. We drove home in silence.

Back home, Rose asked to see my parents and courteously thanked them for their hospitality. She asked to phone for a taxi, then fetched her bag and coat. She ignored me all the time. Five minutes later, the taxi arrived, and she left, saying goodbye to Octavia, but not to me.

'Has nursey gone?' asked my father. 'That little dalliance doesn't seem to have lasted long. But what can you expect if you must start romances with such an unsuitable person? A nurse, for heaven's sake. And a low-grade district nurse from the sticks. Were you that desperate? But I expect your injury has turned your brain. I can fit you up with any number of women.

I'll get you some to be serious with, or if you prefer to go to bed with them, there are plenty who make that their business. Was that the problem with little nursey? Didn't she want you between the sheets? Was your leg too much for even her coarsened sensibilities?'

I would have hit him, and came close to doing so, but I was tired of him, and there were things I wanted from him first, so I checked my temper and went up to my bedroom, where I cried into my pillow.

I did not see my parents again until dinner. I had to be there in order to tell them of Dr Martin's diagnosis. Octavia was excused dinner and told to eat in her room, leaving me free to explain all I had been told. They listened and said they would find a proper doctor in Harley Street. This rash had been exaggerated out of all proportion. I listened. Octavia was my sister, but their daughter, and there was nothing I could do to defy them. I could only hope they would settle on a doctor – no doubt one with a knighthood – who knew his stuff, one who would agree with the diagnosis two other doctors had already given.

'Father,' I said, 'there's something I'd like to ask. When I was in Hallinhag House, I grew interested in its history. And that has sparked off an interest in the history of the family firm.'

'That is unlike you, Dominic.' My father impaled several spears of asparagus on his fork. I cannot imagine where he gets them from, given the season and wartime conditions.

'I have fully made my mind up to enter the firm. I think it will suit me better than any other work, especially with how things are for me now.'

'Really? Well, if you are sincere, no doubt you can be accommodated. Don't you think so, my dear?'

My mother looked up from lifting her own asparagus on to her plate.

'What? Oh, yes, of course, darling. He may be suited to it, and it will keep the business in family hands.'

He looked back at me.

'Of course, you'll have to start as a junior, I'm sure you understand that. But I will provide you with another Portuguese teacher. I consider that important, so we can communicate with associates who don't speak English.'

'I'll go along with whatever you say, Father. There's just one thing. Because of my interest in our early years, I'd like to look over any papers we may have relating to our activities in Portugal and England. I might even be able to put together a brief history of the firm. That could be of interest to our customers.'

I thought he would tell me the family papers were off bounds or that they had been destroyed, but he did not.

'Very well. I'm going in to the office tomorrow. We have an archivist, Cecil Blanchard. I'll ask him to explain what's what. I never paid any attention to that side of things myself. But if it improves your loyalty to the firm, why not?'

He had just reached out for another slice of beef when we heard something from upstairs. Octavia was screaming at the top of her lungs. It went on and on for over a minute. I told my parents to stay and headed upstairs myself.

Friday, 3 January

I spent most of the morning moping about the flat. I was tired, of course, having been up with Octavia. My mother was with me part of the time, but my father just put her screaming down to the air raid that had come later than usual last night. I knew it wasn't the bombing. I knew Octavia scarcely heard it, even with her hearing aid in place. I knew better than anyone that something was in the house.

When my mother left the room to have an early breakfast and see to her toilette – about which she is fastidious, of course – I sat on the edge of the bed and wrote on a notepad for Octavia.

'Why did you scream last night, dear?' I asked.

'I told you,' she wrote on the next sheet. 'Someone is here in the flat.'

'Do you know who?'

She shook her head and wrote.

'Not one of the children. A man, I think. He speaks to me, but I don't understand the words he uses. Do you know who he is?'

'No,' I said, 'but I saw him at the house, I think. I'm trying to find out who he is. But I want to know why you screamed. You don't normally scream, and never so loudly. Did you see him, is that what it was?'

She hesitated.

'I had a bad dream. People were dancing. They had soot on their faces and none of them had feet and some of them had no arms, and in the dream I could hear properly: drums were beating and a man's voice sang words I couldn't understand, and his voice went up and down, and I saw a great mist that came down and covered the dancers, but I could still hear the drumming and the man's voice, and then it was still and I heard nothing, just as if my deafness had returned, and when I woke I was still deaf.'

I thought of my Morris men with their black faces, dancing as they formed a ring about me.

'Did they ring bells?' I asked.

She seemed unsure, so I picked up the little bell she sometimes uses to summon help in the middle of the night. I put it by her ear and she turned up the volume on her aid, and I rang it. She shuddered and nodded, the memory awakened deep inside her.

I went to my room and came back to her, bringing with me my Portuguese guitar. I remembered how I had promised to play it for Rose, and it cut me through and through to think I might never do that now. But I wanted to play for Octavia, something I had never done before. If she could not understand speech yet, surely she could appreciate music. I started with a piece for guitar by Fernando Lopes-Graça, a *partita* which I had adapted for the twelve-string instrument. She'd heard a little music in church, and now I saw her face as she struggled to make sense of it. It did not happen right away, and I had worked my way through three other composers before I saw her eyes light up and a smile come to her lips. I thought I might have found a way to her soul, but I did not ask about such a thing. The damned do not have souls. I looked at the lesions on her face and body and was sure they had grown.

In the afternoon, I went to our offices in High Holborn. My father was busy when I arrived, but I was made welcome and taken to a small, elegantly furnished room and given a cup of green tea, something that must have become hard to get. There were *quejadinhas* from Évora too. Or perhaps someone had baked them from a recipe. They tasted good. I sat down to wait for my father when he was free. To my surprise, he arrived in my little room ten minutes later, bringing with him a man I had not seen before. I tried to stand, rather clumsily I must admit, but he insisted on my staying seated.

The stranger was introduced to me as Cecil Blanchard.

'Cecil is something of an institution here, Dominic. I'm surprised you haven't met him before. Cecil has a phenomenal memory, don't you Cecil?'

'I really can't remember, sir,' said Cecil in a quiet sort of voice.

'Of course,' my father said, 'he is also something of a wit. His formal position in the company is that of archivist. He can pluck out a long-buried document from any point in the two hundred years we have been trading. He knows the names – the names of the people and the names of the ships, he knows the vintage years, two or three per decade, we are terribly fussy, as you know. Tell me, just what is it you're after here? In the murky depths of our history, what do you seek? A *billet-doux*? The diaries of your grandfather's mistress, or his father's paramour or his father's bit on the side? No? What can possibly interest you among all those dusty scrolls tied with pink ribbon? Surely you are not planning to become a historian?'

Sensing that I was about to turn on him, Father addressed himself to Mr Blanchard.

'Cecil, will you please take my son down to the cellars where you keep our sad little collection of invoices and receipts, bills of lading and manifests?'

He turned back to me.

'I'm afraid, Dominic, you'll not find much down there. I should put a handkerchief across your mouth, for there is a lot of dust.'

I thanked him, and Blanchard and I shot off as fast as I could manage. He produced a large key from his pocket and took me to the ground floor, where he showed me a heavy door that sported long iron hinges.

'It won't be easy getting you down here,' he said.

He opened the door, and I saw a narrow staircase that turned as it went down.

'To tell you the truth, a basement is never the best place to keep an archive like this. We constantly have to protect it from damp. I learned a few tricks when I worked at the British

Museum library, but there was a time when none of those things were implemented. Some items have been lost irretrievably.'

'Haven't you tried to move the archive?'

He shook his head.

'May I be completely honest?'

'Of course. Nothing will reach my father.'

'Well, sir, I've gone to your father several times over the years and told him the archive's at risk. He just snaps at me and says I must do as I can. I think he would prefer to see the archive destroyed sooner than preserve it properly.'

I told him what I was looking for.

'That shouldn't be too hard, sir. When I started here, I saw that the oldest papers were most at risk, so I moved them to the safest part of the basement. You say you want documents about Hallinhag House?'

I nodded and he went inside and down. I left the door agape and went off to find a little office for myself on the ground floor. One of the secretaries, a middle-aged woman with spectacles and her hair tied up in a bun, and a pencil stuck inside it as if in a bird's nest, saw me struggling past, guessed who I was, and turned a young woman out of her office to let me use her desk.

Blanchard took his time. I'd been told he was thorough, so I didn't grow too impatient. A junior brought me another cup of tea and a second plate of *quesadinhas*.

'Or perhaps you'd prefer a glass of port, sir. I can fetch you a single *quinta* vintage from 1931, our finest year in some time.'

'Take the tea away,' I said, 'and let me have the port. I had a little of that vintage a few years ago, and it was scrumptious. You should pour a glass for yourself. Bring it here and we'll share it together.'

I reckoned that, if I was to become a port baron, it was time I started to know some of our employees. We sat drinking our port

– and it was every bit as delicious as I remembered, even more so when drunk with the little cakes – while we chatted. He told me about his wife – they were newly married – and the little property they rented, and by the time he finished I thought I understood him, his problems and what he wanted to do in his life.

Over an hour had passed when Cecil Blanchard returned, carrying several boxes. My port-drinking companion made his excuses and left, taking the bottle with him. I told him to take it home to share with his wife, who is a stenographer at the War Ministry. Father will never miss it.

The next two hours passed surprisingly quickly. Blanchard had extracted all the early documents relating to Hallinhag, but had also brought along a box of papers that told the story of the founding of the firm, its first imports to London, and some bits and pieces about my family: letters, a wedding certificate, some burial notices, and even part of a diary, similar to the one I am keeping today.

I only left because of the curfew, and then most reluctantly. At first the papers were jumbled, and many were hard to read. Gradually, however, with Blanchard's help, a pattern began to emerge. Port came from Oporto in small shipments to begin with, during the 1730s and 1740s. It was stored in a shed on the East London Docks. At that time, the family had other businesses, manufacturing ropes for naval ships and importing cotton, silk and tea from India as shareholders in the East India Company. They were also involved with the Company in the trade in opium from Bengal to China.

The head of my family at that time was Sir Henry Lancaster. At the age of thirty-five, he married the Honourable Lucy Craven, who bore four children for him and promptly died. Lucy came from a very respectable family that had a magnificent house in the Lake District, Marlowe Hall. There, the happy couple – if they were indeed happy – had spent many weeks each year, but in 1731 a fire broke out that gutted the house far beyond repair. Blanchard showed me a full account of the event, what had become of the staff, and how the loss of the Hall had broken Lucy's father's heart. He had set great store by the building, which had been designed at the start of the century when Wren and Hawksmoor were still in partnership, and which had contained furniture and *objets d'art* of great cost and surprising beauty.

Sir Henry ordered the construction of Hallinhag House, a much smaller establishment, as a temporary dwelling for his parents-in-law, who were settling into their London house for the coming season. They never lived there, but when visiting during its construction Lord Craven went swimming in Ullswater one Sunday afternoon and never returned to shore. They found his shoes, his shirt and his breeches on the rock where he had left them. His body was never recovered. His widow decided to remain in London.

And so Hallinhag became the Lancaster family's summer resort. At about that time, Sir Henry was looking for a business that could be run closer to home. The long distances to and from India, and the precarious nature of the opium trade, which was illegal in China, led him to think of Portugal, with its long history in trade and exploration in the East, and this led him to port and the development of the vineyards in the upper Douro region. Thus Lancaster ports were born.

Sir Henry died in 1761, but the trade was continued under the auspices of his son William, who strengthened links with Portugal. He himself spent some time in the country, returning in 1745 to marry his old sweetheart, the honourable Jane Fitzgibbons, whose grave I now remember seeing in the churchyard at St Martin's.

It is about this time that we found something untoward. I haven't been able to piece it all together, but I can guess at some of it.

Here is the text of a letter written by William soon after he took over the family fortunes.

Hallinghag House
Ullswater

His Grace the Duke of Westmoreland
My Lord Duke,
I wish to thank Yr Grace for Yr latest communication. It is a relief to know that her Ladyship is fully recovered from her late illness. We have weathered great storms in these past few years, have we not, m'Lord?

I take pleasure to inform Yr Grace that the shipment of Colheitas that was promised last year has arrived safely after having aged in oak barrels for these past 20 years. This firft shipment amounts to only fifty bottles, of which I have taken the immense liberty to reserve two dozen for Yr Grace, together with a barrel of Garrafeira for the Cambridge Club, where it will be laid down for above two years. A second vessel will dock in London in the next week, barring foul weather, with what we know on board. If this supply be healthy, as we anticipate, it will give some breathing space here at Ullswater.

Last week, we lost three to ye gas or to whatsoever else was brought here by ye dancing men. I have asked Dr — to attend us, but after the last time he pleads business elsewhere. Perhaps Yr Grace can persuade him as You best know how and have the mood for it and the temperament. I defer to Yr Grace's wisdom in all such matters, and I herewith enclose a bag of what you know in order to entice Yr Grace's appetite for more. May I inquire if the young lady I sent last month has proved satisfactory? The supply of such goods is almost limitless, but it must be kept dark.

Did Sir Q— receive what they sent from Lisbon, that came out of China by way of Cairo? He is too dmn'd fastidious and has no knowledge of what else we do here.

As ever in this matter, m'Lord, I rely on Yr discretion. Should Yr Grace wish to inspect for Yourself what work we carry on here, I pledge myself to see to all Yr needs, for there is much to be seen, though they be restless both day and night. But rest assured they can be pacified. The ones who dance go at their japes & antiques something marvellous. They beat their drums and clash their sticks like the brute savages they are, and their black faces are a terror to me.

Believe me at all times, my Lord, with sincerity and respect, your faithful obliged and humble servant,

William Lancaster Bart

There were other letters of a similar tenor. All of them light, many of them cross-letters, where the writing of one page is written over diagonally by what follows, in order to save money. Cecil Blanchard explained to me that in that period it was the recipient who paid for post, not the sender, and that heavier and longer letters attracted higher fees. I found these letters hard to read, but I have brought some home in order to apply myself more thoroughly to them. The letters were often in Sir William's hand and had been returned to him for reasons I could not guess. They do not seem to have been unwelcome, for sometimes the original recipients would add friendly notes in a margin or near the signature. William's addressees included the Honourable Bertram Grisham, the Marquess of Mallen, the Earl of Dunlop, the Viscount Newton, the Bishop of Durham, and less exalted men – there were no women – such as Sir Waldo Featherstone, Mr John Hawkridge, the Master of Rivenhall, and a number of individuals whom I took to be tradesmen.

This correspondence took place over an extended compass. From one in Scotland, to two in Devon, to another in Yorkshire, one in Northumberland, and several in London. There were also several letters to him from Portugal, some from Lisbon, others from Oporto or Porto, and one from Coimbra, which is a prestigious university town like Oxford or Cambridge.

Later

I have just finished my first examination of these documents at home. They lie on the table like feathers that may, if stroked firmly enough, transform themselves back into birds. Nothing is straightforward. The letters are of very different dates: Cecil explained that it was not the custom then to include the year. There are various bills and receipts, only a few of which relate to shipments or sales of port. Some are for building materials, some are more obscure, like two in Portuguese that carry the tally of *dez es'os*, which I can't disentangle save for the 'ten' at the start. Perhaps we can find someone who can read Portuguese better than I, since there are several letters, a few ship's manifests, and a sort of diary in that language. Cecil tells me he will look for someone at London University. Unfortunately, nobody's there at the moment since the whole university has moved out to safer locations round the country. The Ministry of Information has moved in. Cecil tells me King's College has moved out to several destinations, Bristol, Glasgow, Birmingham and Leeds. We'll have to work out who can tell us where their Portuguese department has gone – if they still have one, that is.

I have organized the papers as best I can for the moment. One thing that has surprised me is a list of names, Portuguese names. The main list is organized alphabetically, and has asterisks against five names. It reads like this:

Adão★
Agostinho
Alícia
Caetano Moura
Clara★
Clarissa
Débora
Dinis
Érica
Félix
Geraldo Paredes
Gilberto Ribeiro
Helena★
Hugo
Irene
Loão
Margarida★
Mateus
Octávia★
Paulo
Raymundo
Rebeca

It is the names with asterisks that frighten me. I was at first quite indifferent to them until I looked more closely. Adão. Clara. Helena. Margarida. Octávia. Adam. Clare. Helen. Margaret. And Octavia. Not English girls at all, not an English boy. Portuguese children, all of them, except for my sister. Unless my father had conceived her with a Portuguese woman during one of his long business trips to the country. Octavia did not in the least resemble my mother, who remained indifferent to her. My sister is dark-haired and looks as Portuguese as an Infanta.

Later

I was working on the documents in the library, where the family books – several generations' worth – are kept, along with technical materials about wine, port, viniculture and Portugal. It is my favourite room in the flat, and over the years I have taken pains to keep it in good repair and to ensure that everything is maintained in good order. I was starting to feel hungry and realized it must be close to dinner. At that moment, the door opened and my mother appeared. She seemed a little on edge.

'Dominic,' she said, 'have you seen Octavia lately?'

'No,' I said, shaking my head. 'Not for some hours. I thought she stayed here today.'

'Well, yes, she did. She had lunch, then went up to her bedroom for a nap. She didn't come down for tea, and I thought she had either fallen fast asleep or hadn't heard the gong. But just now, when I went up to get her ready for dinner, she wasn't in her room. I've asked around, but nobody has seen her. She's very thick with Mrs Mayberry, but when I asked her just now, she hadn't seen hide nor hair of her. Your father has been into every room, but there's no sign of her anywhere in the apartment.'

'Could she have just popped out?'

'What for? All the shops are shut. It's curfew time, and if there's to be a raid, it may not be far off.'

'Mother, help me up the stairs. I want to look at her room.'

It didn't take me long to find what was wrong.

'Her coat is missing, and her scarf. She normally keeps her gloves in this drawer.' I opened it. Her latest gloves, given to her at Christmas, were gone. Her boots were always lined up beside her shoes, but now they too had disappeared.

'Does she have money?' I asked.

I turned round to see my father in the door.

'As a matter of fact, yes, she does,' he said. 'She asked for some yesterday, enough for a new dress, something by Hardy Amies, she said. I didn't think Amies did clothes for little girls, but she assured me she'd seen a dress the right size just down on Oxford Street. She told me you'd promised to take her and get her back here all right. Did you make some damn-fool promise?'

'Of course I didn't, and I'd appreciate it if you didn't level accusations before you know the facts. She has taken us all in.'

Just then my mother bent down and came up holding a white envelope.

'This must have fallen off the bedside table,' she said.

It was addressed to me. Mother passed it over and I opened it.

Dear Dominic,
Have gone to fetch Rosie back. I can't bear not to have her here.
She doesn't seem to like you much, but you have to do your best
and make her like you again. Have some money for train. Won't
be long. Don't wait up.

I read it and passed it to my father, who was already apoplectic.

'I said there'd be trouble if you got involved with that slut. What is the stupid child thinking? She can't get far on what I gave her.'

But I knew Octavia was cleverer than that. She'd put a label round her neck, addressing herself to Rose in Pooley Bridge, and once on the train she'd find a way of asking for help. They'd treat her as a lost evacuee, and someone would be sure to be going her way. I told my parents we should expect a letter or a telephone call tomorrow or the day after.

My father snorted and stormed off. Our brief *entente* had come to an end.

My mother picked up the note from where my father had thrown it to the floor.

'Your father's angry. Quite understandably. Give him time to think.'

There was no point in my setting off in the middle of the curfew. The first ARP warden to set eyes on me would have sent me straight home with a flea or two in my ear. And there would have been no train.

I put my things together before going to bed, including a small case with the documents I had retrieved yesterday. To be honest, I was worried about Octavia. Although she was resourceful, I knew she was also quite trusting, and in wartime it paid to have your wits about you. Her handicap could lead to problems unless she found one or two people to help her. But it wasn't a straightforward journey, and people at the start might not understand her final destination.

I left at first light in a taxi, leaving a note on the hall table, and pushed my way on to the first train. Getting out of London wasn't too bad. There were a lot of weekend passes, so soldiers and airmen were packing the inward-bound trains. By the time I got to Birmingham, it was every man for himself, but my leg secured me a good seat all the way.

For my own part, I was furious with Octavia. Rose had made her intentions clear, and I had no idea how to explain what had happened or relieve her mistrust of me. I'd much rather have stayed in London, but Octavia had forced my hand. What was I going to say to Rose and her mother when I got to Pooley Bridge?

It was impossible to read my papers on the train. There just

172

wasn't enough room, and trying to hold them across my knees was hopeless, especially since my left leg (or what was left of it) could give way at any second. I had found a book about the port wine trade in the library and devoured it instead. I could feel the taste of the port I was given yesterday, the single *quinta* vintage, as it had lain on my tongue for hours after I tasted it. Someday, I thought, I would have to sit down with one of the company's tasters and ask him to teach me how to develop a palate.

I arrived in Pooley Bridge by bus from Penrith. I had brought little luggage, and I came equipped with only my stick. It was, thank God, a stout specimen, and it held my weight every time I shifted from foot to false leg. I made my way directly to Dr Raverat's house, thinking it might be best to consult him before turning up at the Sansoms'.

He was delighted to see me, declared that he'd missed me bitterly, and hoped my time in London had passed well.

'In some ways, yes,' I said, in reply to this last remark. We were still standing on the doorstep.

'I take it you're on your way to Rose's place. I'd get there smartish if I were you. I think they get to bed early, now you're not around to drag them out at midnight.'

'The truth is, Doctor, I'm a little apprehensive about going there. Would it trouble you if I came in and chatted over a cup of tea?'

He was all smiles at this and snatched my little case up the better to sweep me in.

Once the tea was brewing on the table, we sat down.

'Tell me all,' he said.

I told him about introducing Rose to my parents and my father's wrath. Then I described how I had discovered the papers

I'd brought up, and why I hoped to find some sort of explanation in them that might provide a solution to the manifestations at Hallinhag House. Finally, I told him why I had returned so early, that Octavia, following her definitive diagnosis, had left the apartment and headed north.

'Do you know if she got here safely?' I asked.

He shook his head.

'I haven't seen her, but she would have arrived late and I was out last night till midnight, with an emergency up on the fells. I've been busy all today as well. But why did she want to come back here without you?'

There was nothing for it but to tell him.

'Doctor, your job must bring you into contact with all sorts of curious and shameful behaviour. You may not like me when I have told you this, but I need to anyway.'

And so I told him about Rose and myself, making it seem that I had seduced her and not the other way round. I then told him about what had happened, about the creature or vision, the rough skin; how I had pushed Rose away, on to the floor, and that she had not spoken to me since. He listened without displaying emotion, and when I had finished smiled.

'Dominic, first, please don't put yourself through this guilt. There's a war on, and ninety percent of the adult population is having sexual relations, whether inside or outside marriage. Your intentions towards Rose are perfectly sound, and there's no reason you shouldn't have a perfectly happy life.'

'But I shouldn't have taken advantage of her.'

Her laughed out loud.

'Dominic, I've known Rose all her life. If she slept with you, it's because she wanted to. I suspect she had more to do with it than you. Am I right?'

I knew he was right, and nodded my head.

'But she thinks I violently, cruelly, rejected her . . .'

'Listen, I want to check on Octavia, and while I'm there I'll find a chance to talk to Rose. Once she knows what really happened she'll welcome you back.'

So it turned out. He was away for almost an hour, and when he came back he grinned and said he'd spoken to her privately and told her everything.

'And now she wants you back. She knows she must have hurt you, but leaving was all she could think of at the time.'

So I took my case and left, and when I knocked at the cottage door, Rose opened it and her face told me everything.

'I was in bed,' she said, 'when the doctor called, and I was more unhappy than I've ever been, and unsure if I'd done the right thing, but frightened of you and frightened of myself, and . . .'

I cut her off by bending forward and kissing her, and so eager was I that I forgot to hold my stick in place, with the result that I toppled over and fell on the threshold, banging my head on the doorstep. When I next looked up, she was there, holding me by the arms and pulling me up. Then she moved to one side, and there was Octavia holding my stick.

'She was distressed when I left London,' said Rose, 'so she got herself up here. She'll tell you all about her journey tomorrow. I know you'll want to tell her off, but go easy on her. She was very brave. And I already know what things were like in your flat. I will never forgive your father for what he said.'

'Can I come in?' I said. 'It's freezing out here.'

I gave Octavia a hug, and as I did so I noticed that her rough skin had grown in area.

We arranged a meeting this afternoon, to be held in the Reverend Braithwaite's vicarage, and I presented the materials I'd brought up from London. It was all of great interest, but no one could make a stab at the more important questions or say whether or not they were related to the troubles in Hallinhag House. I knew I would have to go back there before long, but I wanted to be armed with as much information as possible. We gave up in time to get home before curfew. Before he dropped us at Rose's door, Dr Raverat drove me to his surgery where I hurriedly telephoned Cecil Blanchard, and then made a second call to my father, instructing him to authorize Blanchard to take a week's leave and to pay him all he might need for a return journey to Penrith and a week's lodging in Pooley Bridge. He made no complaint.

Some of the letters were of greater interest than others. One gave us cause for great concern.

My Dear Sir William,

The obligations, and many instances of affection, which I have received from Yr Honour, do engage to make returns suitable to your merits. But although I have this set home upon my spirit, I may not (shall I tell you, I cannot?) obtain the same workings as previously until more months have elapsed, and I entreat Yr Honour's patience in all matters concerning this. And herein it is my purpose, as soon as I can remove impediments, and some weights that press me down, to make a farther progress, and discharge my promise to your Honour in relation to that.

And now I shall come to return Yr Honour thanks for your judicious choice of that Person to whom you have entrufted our weightieft Affair: an Affair wherein Yr Honour is concerned, though not in an equal degree and measure with myself. I muſt confess that I had some doubts of its success, till Providence cleared them to me by the effects. I was, truly, and to speak ingenuously, not without doubtings; and shall not be ashamed to give Yr Honour the grounds I had for much doubting. I did fear that Senhor Ameixoeiro would not have been able to go through and carry on that work; and that either the Duke would have cooled in his suit, or condescended to his Brother. I doubted also that those Instructions which I sent over were not clear enough as to expressions; some affairs here denying me leisure at that time to be so particular as, to some circumstances, I would. – If I am not mistaken in his character, as I received it from your Eminency, that fire which is kindled between them will not want bellows to blow it, and keep it burning.

And ſo, Yr Honour, to more immediate matters and the consequences of Yr Instructions this laſt month. A large ſhipment of port has left Lisbon in these past few days, wherein Yr Honour will find included six barrels of ruby, a barrel each of Colheita and Garrafeira, ſome vintage that has been late bottled by Maſter Barouqueiro, two barrels of tawny from the Quinta of Senhora Pontes, in the Cima Corgo. Yr Honour should take care to taste this last wine in particular. It is a mix of the grapes of Touriga Franca, Touriga Nasional and Tinta Roriz, together with others, and you will find in it the flavours of maple, raisins and blackberries combined with dark chocolate and a hint of spices. It is one of our most splendid ports, I do assure Yr Honour.

In the matter of slaves (escravos), Senhor Carvalho has made enquiries in Lisbon. We have found a full dozen according to your specifications, that were bound for Brazil but may as well remain here in Portugal. All are sound of limb and body, and none suffers from the malignancy that has wasted so many of your previous slaves. Some come from Angola, others from the

177

*lands of the Hausa. They are tall and strong and already have
experience at hard work. You will not be disappointed. They
may last a good nine months or more.*

*Beyond that, I must apprise Yr Honour that I have secured
four children for Yr Purposes. Their names are Adão, Clara,
Helena and Margarida. They are fine and healthy children,
unlike the others whom I ſent before, and will, in good faith, be
to Yr Honour's liking.*

*If I have troubled your Honour too long in this, you may
impute it to the reſentment of joy which I have for the issue of
this Affair; and will conclude with giving you aſſurance that I
will never be backward in demonstrating, as becomes your friend
and confederate, that I am, Your humble servant, Theodore
Wilkinson.*

Rose and I have been released from our short nightmare, but I
am still uneasy in my heart. How did the four children come to
be seen on Cherry Holm? Are the black dancers of my dreams
the same as Octavia's Portuguese slaves of the letters, men taken
from a colony or Cape Verde or the Congo? Or are they black-
faced Morris dancers performing a stick dance, figures from a
childhood memory, something I must have seen in Portugal
and described to Octavia? Do they dance the *Dança dos Paus*,
the Portuguese Dance of the Sticks that the Pauliteiros dance?
Are the children in the house William's Portuguese children?
Why were they sent to him? There are too many questions, and
I know so little.

Rose and I spent the end of the day walking slowly along the
lake shore, holding hands and kissing from time to time. We
carried memories of passion, but could have no satisfaction, and,
to be honest, both of us were afraid to rouse whatever had come
between us in London.

When we got back, Octavia was waiting for us. She had been helping Jeanie prepare supper. Her jigsaw lay on the kitchen table, where it would soon be covered up by a linen tablecloth.

We ate a good dinner, and when the table was cleared Octavia went back to her jigsaw. Jeanie asked us to step into the parlour to listen to the wireless. She switched to the Home Service and came in early to a speech by Mr Churchill.

We stood our ground and faced the two Dictators in the hour of what seemed their overwhelming triumph, and we have shown ourselves capable, so far, of standing up against them alone. After the heavy defeats of the German air force by our fighters in August and September, Herr Hitler did not dare attempt the invasion of this Island, although he had every need to do so and although he had made vast preparations. Baffled in this grandiose project, he sought to break the spirit of the British nation by the bombing, first of London, and afterwards of our great cities.

We can never listen enough to Mr Churchill, he does us proud every time. I don't know what that evil bastard Hitler says in his speeches, but they can never be as fine or as eloquent as the words of our Leader.

Jeanie turned the radio off once the speech came to an end. There was silence for a while. My heart was beating. Rose and I sat together on the sofa. Outside, a wind had risen, and I knew that if I walked down to the lake, I would find it tossed and angry. A German plane flew overhead, on its way to Barrow. And the wind was solemn, without pity.

'Mother,' said Rose. Her voice quavered. 'I have some-thing to tell you. That's to say, Dominic and I need to tell you something.'

179

'Not more ghosts, I hope?' Jeanie said, partly making light of it.

'Not ghosts, Mam. You've guessed by now, I'm sure.'

'Oh, you can be sure I have. Waltzing around with the vicar, sitting snug together as you are now. Have you set a date?'

'Not yet. But not too long. First, Dominic has to sort out his house at Howtown. After that, I think.'

'And what about you, Mr Lancaster?' Jeanie Sansom was a shrewd woman: she'd not let me off lightly if I wanted to marry her daughter. Her love for Rose was passionate, perhaps as strong as mine, and she would not let her go to just anyone.

'What about me?'

'What do your Mum and Dad think of this? Or haven't you told them yet?'

I shook my head.

'I have told them. But I won't tell you what they said in return. I would not want to hurt you or Rose. Rose was there. She has seen my father behave like Hitler. We shall marry without their blessing. I will take Octavia's happiness for us as sufficient for my family.'

'That's enough for me. Now, tell me what happened to you in London.'

Monday, 6 January

We went to church this morning, and afterwards I had a long chat with the Reverend Braithwaite. He was intrigued by what I had brought back from London.

'I had a dream,' I said. We were walking by the lakeside while a gentle snow fell like a benediction. He had prayed for his parishioners, alive and dead. Behind us came Rose and Octavia.

'Not one dream,' I said, 'but several. And Octavia has had the same dream. I think it belongs to the dead.'

I told him about my dream of black-faced men dancing and using sticks, as in a Morris dance. 'Sometimes their legs are severed, sometimes whole. They bob up and down. I can hear the clicking of their sticks.'

'Dominic,' he said, 'there is an Anglican parish of Nova Lima in the state of Minas Gerais in Brazil, where they have gold mines. There used to be more slaves in that region than any other in Brazil. A friend of mine, Iain Cameron, lived there for several years. He stayed with me here after he returned. He told me that when there were still slaves there they danced a dance called *maculelé*, in which they struck sticks against one another, exactly as they do in the stick Morris dances. And their faces are black. And the blacks there still dance the *maculelé*.'

'Do you think William's slaves danced like that in Portugal?'

'Perhaps. Perhaps. Now, I think we've made ourselves cold enough. Let's get Rose and Octavia back inside.'

Dr Raverat had arranged to collect us after visiting a patient, and so I could update him on my finds in a calmer manner than I was able to last night.

Tonight, Octavia fell ill. She started as if she had contracted a cold, and I regretted having allowed her outside in this cold snap. It didn't seem serious enough for me to call on Dr Raverat again, but Rose said I should keep an eye on her. We put her to bed at nine, and I stayed with her for a while and tried to distract her with some stories, which I told with my fingers. I thought she would fall asleep, but as I gestured to her I noticed she was growing more uncomfortable and was starting a fever. I called Rose, who examined her carefully and took her temperature.

'Her fever is getting quite high,' she said. 'I just had a reading of one hundred and two. We can leave her to sweat it out, but I'm worried there could be a link to her leprosy. I don't know enough to say if it could be a symptom or not.'

'What else could it be?'

She shrugged.

'I really don't know. There are some odd symptoms.'

'Couldn't it just be a result of her being out in the cold today?'

She shook her head.

'It's not impossible, but I don't think so. She said earlier that she had aches in her joints. When I examined her just now, I found swollen glands in her groin. And the fever seems unusually severe. I want to bring the fever down if I can.'

We found the cottage bath and moved it to Octavia's room, which was where I slept as well. Rose made an infusion of yarrow; she said she often used it on patients and found it effective. It took a lot of kettles, but we got the bath half-filled with the infusion. Rose undressed Octavia and I helped lift her into the bath. We left her there for a while, watching her the whole time and adding some hot water as the infusion grew cold. When it was all done, we put her nightdress back on and slipped her into bed with a hot-water bottle against the cold.

Wednesday, 8 January

Cecil Blanchard arrived today at noon. He'd spoken to my father on Monday, who loaned him a small car – not the Hispano – to make the journey up to the Lakes. He began the tiring journey yesterday, but he decided to break it in Sheffield, doing the rest today.

Before his arrival, we had woken early to check on Octavia.

182

Her fever had gone down, but was still high, and Rose continued to be uneasy. She went to fetch Dr Raverat as soon as it was reasonable to do so. He hurried here, still unshaven and without a tie. Snow was still falling, there was a silence of birds. He came in, brushing white flakes from his shoulders. I watched him as if from afar. His presence altered things, made Octavia's case seem more dangerous. He and Rose talked for several minutes, then she led him to where Octavia lay in bed. The child had fallen back into a fitful sleep. Rose took her temperature and looked at the stick.

'It has gone back up again,' she said.

Dr Raverat had brought a sphygmomanometer and stethoscope, which he used to assess her blood pressure and lungs. He shook his head as he pulled back from the bed.

'I'd like to get her to hospital,' he said. 'I don't recognize her symptoms.'

He turned to Rose.

'You say she had a headache overnight and dizziness this morning.'

'That's right. I don't understand. Nothing fits together.'

'I'm as perplexed as you are. I'm going to ring through to Barrow and get them to send an ambulance over.'

'Is she in any danger, Doctor?' I asked. 'I'll never forgive myself if anything happens to her. I forced her to make the journey back here.'

He put his hand on my arm.

'Nobody forced her. But I'll not keep this from you. Octavia does give me cause for alarm. Years ago, I'd have given up on her the minute I set eyes on her face and listened to her chest. But we have these new sulfa drugs now, which can work miracles. The hospital in Barrow has a super new drug called Prontosil. It's used mainly on members of the armed forces. I daresay they gave you a dose or two on board that hospital ship.'

183

Rose nodded. She had my notes, which she kept well hidden.

'You had an infection in your wound,' she said. 'Prontosil probably saved your life.'

Raverat took himself off, back to his surgery, for he had a long list of patients to see that morning. He told Rose to fetch him when the ambulance came, and said he might travel to the North Lonsdale with Octavia.

'I only wish it weren't so damned cold. She'll have a rough ride if they can't make time.'

By noon the ambulance had not arrived. At ten minutes past, Blanchard turned up with a screech of brakes. When we went out to greet him, we found the snow lying heavily and more coming down. It was not quite a blizzard, but it was not far off. He told us he hadn't been sure he was going to get through.

I asked Blanchard to wait inside, and Rose helped me across to Dr Raverat's house. The waiting room was still packed with patients, young and old. Several had colds or the first signs of the 'flu, and one old woman looked too frail to have ventured out in this weather.

Dr Raverat saw us when he came out from his previous patient.

'Have they picked her up yet?' he asked. 'I couldn't get over – you can see how busy it has been. There'll be more in the afternoon.'

We told him the ambulance still had not arrived.

His face flushed, and he went back inside the consulting room. I could hear him using the telephone.

When he came out, he looked angry.

'Damn it to hell,' he exploded. I thought I was back in the Navy.

'What's happening?'

'Nothing. Absolutely nothing. They say the roads are closed for miles around. They have farmers out to bring in as many sheep as possible. It's a national emergency, and they say there's no chance of an ambulance getting to Pooley Bridge and back. I should have driven her myself while there was still a chance of getting through. If only I could lay my hands on that sulfa drug.'

Back at Rose's cottage, Octavia was declining. I found Jeanie with Cecil Blanchard sitting on either side of her bed.

'The ambulance isn't coming,' I said. 'That means she won't get the medicine Dr Raverat prescribed for her. We'll just have to make do with what we have. He'll be over again later.'

'You'll need to ring your father,' Cecil said. 'Do you have a telephone here?'

I shook my head and, leaving Rose to get Blanchard settled in, I struggled to the Post Office.

'I'm sorry, dear,' said the Postmistress, 'but all the lines have just gone down. I'd suggest a telegram, but they've been suspended for the duration, as you probably know.'

Rose demanded quiet in the bedroom and shooed her mother, Cecil and myself into the parlour. Jeanie, who was tearful after watching how Octavia was sinking, shuffled off to the kitchen. She would need extra rations for Cecil, but he had handed her his book.

Cecil and I talked about Octavia for a while. A periously ill child was not what he'd expected to find at the end of his exhausting trip. I ended up telling him much more about Hallinhag House than I'd intended. Then we kept vigil by burying ourselves in the documents: the ones I had brought here and others that he had found in the archive on Monday.

I took him through the letters I had read. There were several in Portuguese that I did not understand. He put these to one side and said he'd brought a Portuguese–English dictionary with him and, better still, an ancient Portuguese dictionary which had been stuck on a shelf in the office for decades.

185

'My Portuguese isn't too good,' he said, 'but I manage to get by. I'm often asked to translate letters. As you can imagine, it comes in handy from time to time in this business.'

Rose had to help the doctor for the rest of the day, but he told her to stay where she was, in order to look after Octavia, and with instructions to fetch him if she showed significant signs of getting worse. So Rose stayed in the bedroom, trying to bring the fever down. Cecil and I remained in the parlour, where he offloaded his papers on the little table.

Bit by bit we worked through what we had. From time to time Rose would emerge from the bedroom carrying a bowl of linens. 'There's no sign of any improvement,' she said, 'but Octavia's condition has stabilized, and that's a blessing.'

I wondered if Cecil knew of our engagement, and reckoned that my father would most certainly have said nothing to him about us. So I told him, adding 'My father doesn't approve.'

'I expect not, sir. He's not the sort of man to approve of much.' Then he added. 'It's not that I wish to seem disloyal, for your father has kept us going, especially since the war started.'

We bent our heads back to the documents. Bit by bit we disentangled the story of Hallinhag House and its grounds.

William (who had registered the proofs of succession to the baronetcy within three days of his father's death and was now Sir William Lancaster, just as my father holds the baronetcy today) established a growing business selling port to the gentry. His bottles could be found in the salons of every club in Pall Mall, and at one point he started to supply the Great Hall at Hampton Court Palace. The King took a great liking for port and ordered it in barrels for his own use and that of his favoured courtiers.

In 1755, Sir William had his Portuguese secretary write to his agent in Oporto, a man called Luis Carvalho.

Exmo. Senhor Luis,

The children have arrived and we find them to be in good condition. They speak passable English, which I muſt owe to Yr credit, and their names are Adão, Clara, Helena, Margarida; but I have told them that they muſt use English names from now on: Adam, Clare, Helen and Margaret. They will make fine, uncomplaining servants and useful interlocutors with the Brazilians, once they have enough English for it. If they do not, by God! I shall beat it into them. The little girls are pretty enough, and I know that Lord L— and Sir William B— may like to have a discussion with them.

Last night we held a séance, in the course which each of the children in turn communicated with the dead. Some of the voices were in Portugueſe, others in Engliſh, and one in French. I heard them diſtinctly and was sure the children were not weaving a falsehood by adopting unnatural voices. For example, several of the male voices were emitted by the boy, who naturally has a child's voice and cannot achieve the deep register of theſe ghoſts, nor speak of the things he is given to speak of.

Let me know if you have other children like theſe. I have friends who also wish to commune with those who have passed on. It is early days, but I aſſure you theſe children may be the greatest crop yet of the Douro valley. I shall start them for Hallinhag tomorrow, and mean to keep them there for the season. I may bring them to London in due course, for there are several gentlemen in the City that will have of them whereof they know or may discover, for there are as many churchyards and crypts in the metropolis as there are in the entire country combined. There are burial places for kings and queens. Who would not wish to speak with the phantom of Henry or Richard or Mr Cromwell?

Pleaſe let me have the uſual barrels by return. If you have

anything of an oddity, of wines of which we have not tasted,
please convey them.
    De V.Exa.
    Sir William Lancaster Bart

We worked our way through bills of lading, receipts for barrels and bottles of all sizes, orders for material for new offices in High Holborn, and the architect's plans for Hallinhag House. Here we found the missing attic: the plan showed a large space that ran from one side of the house to the other and from front to back. 'I wonder how we'd find it,' I said to Cecil.

'You would need to make measurements,' he said. 'Perhaps it's well concealed.'

I made a note to find some way to check this, perhaps from outside.

It seems the family business was in part made possible by the presence of African slaves. In 1750, Luis Salgado, *'uma pessoa de grande importância'*, wrote to Sir William to explain that instructions had been given for the dispatch to Oporto of six slaves from Benguela and Cabinda, Portuguese colonies in Africa, near Kongo. They helped work the vineyards. Salgado explained that they would last about six months, and that he would supply replacements as soon as they were needed.

There were letters from aristocrats in this country and abroad. At first we thought them part of an elaborate game, but there were too many of them to persuade us for long that that was the case. One ran as follows:

My Dear Sir William,
I wish to thank You, good Sir, for the wit and elegance with
which You coordinated the séance last week. I confess myself to
have been of a fkeptical bent and that I was solely persuaded to

attend the reading by my Lord the Earl of Dunlop, by whose
recommendation I and feveral of my acquaintance have fought
guidance in that quarter. What the children reported from the
ghosts was most uncanny, for my late father did often speak in
such terms, and there were matters that I had heard before only
from my mother. On my return home I related to her what I
had been told and she burft into weeping, for she said it was
like having my father to home again and in his old chair. I have
returned to the graveyard what was taken from it, but can as easily
disinter those same remains should we need further news from
beyond the grave. It is a long journey to your country home, but it
has been a most worthwhile undertaking. Nevertheless, I did find
it disagreeable to travel so far with my father in the coach beside
me. In future, I may carry him in a cart of some kind behind us.
   My sincerest good wishes.
   Lord Trevor

We could stomach no more. Cecil retired, exhausted, and I
went to sit with my sister.

Octavia died as the clock in our room struck midnight. It was
dark outside and the night lay huddled beneath falling sheets of
snow. I had left the curtains folded back, ignoring the blackout.
No planets passed tonight, no moon came down like a silver
disc to kiss the lake, and no stars crackled in the frozen sky
like shards of ice. I had been left alone with her. I watched her
for an hour or more, my hand in hers, cooling her fever with a
facecloth that had been dipped in cold water. I sat with my head
close to hers, listening to her breathing. It was raw and racked
with tiny sobs. She was very still for a long time, and sometimes
I thought she was gone. Then I would hear her breathing and
see her chest rise and fall. Then, quite suddenly, her body flexed

189

itself, lifting her up several inches, then moving back to the bed again. And I heard her speak in barely audible tones, but clear enough for me to hear.

'I . . . can hear . . . them whispering,' she said. 'The children . . . like . . . they did . . . before. Whispering to me . . . to join them . . . I don't want . . . to go . . . but they are . . . forcing me . . .'

She grew silent, but when I listened I could hear them whispering to her, in low tones that I couldn't understand. And that was when she died, on a single breath, while her eyes were closed in darkness and her hand went limp in mine. The heat began to leave her body as if it had never been there.

Thursday, 9 January

Dr Raverat and the Reverend Braithwaite were in the kitchen, sitting with Rose and Jeanie. I fetched them in and said I thought she had stopped breathing. The doctor looked for her pulse and placed a mirror above her lips, and when he had done he pronounced her dead.

I didn't know where to look for grief. It was not in my heart. Death had come as too great a shock. I didn't even know what had killed her, whether it was leprosy or this new, unidentified disease. The ambulance had never come, nor the medicines that might have saved her tiny life. She had passed from life to death as silently as she had lived. Octavia was precious to me beyond words, but I still lay awake some nights with the noises of the Battle of Dakar ringing in my mind. I had seen thousands of men lost at sea, and now I had too little grief in me to mourn my only sister.

Rose wept, and her mother was moved to tears of her own.

Dr Raverat took me aside.

'Dominic, we have a problem. We can't leave Octavia here for long. I would normally have taken her to the mortuary in Barrow, or asked them to fetch her. We need to have a post-mortem, to see if we can get any answers to the question of how she died. But that seems impossible for the present. I don't want to put her in some barn or outbuilding – that would be too undignified. Would your family mind if I asked Oliver Braith-waite if she could be moved to the church in the morning?'

The vicar was very keen to open St Peter's and place her in front of the altar straight away, given the events leading up to her death, but he didn't think we'd make it that far.

'What about Donald McIntyre's little motor launch?' I asked. 'It's still moored near the jetty, isn't it?'

Oliver nodded.

'But we'll have to wake him up,' I thought aloud. 'And he's very fussy about letting other people use his boat.'

'I'll take care of it,' he replied, 'and I'll come with you to the church. Will you be all right for the journey? It's several degrees below freezing.'

'Has the snow stopped? We'll have to run as close to the shore as possible. Come back when you have the matter in hand.'

He left, wrapping himself against the wind. I knew it would be even colder on the lake.

Rose had set about washing Octavia and dressing her in her best nightdress. About half-way through, she stopped and asked Dr Raverat to come across.

'Doctor,' she said, 'something's wrong.'

'I can't see anything.'

'It's what's not there, sir. The leprosy scarring. I can't see any sign of it.'

He put his spectacles on and looked closely. Rose was right: the marks of leprosy had gone.

Fifteen minutes passed. Then the door opened, bringing with it a light flurry of snow. The Reverend Braithwaite came in, stamping his feet and clapping his hands hard together. We let him go to the fire, where he stood for a little while.

'I have good news and bad news,' he said, still chafing his hands together. 'The bad news is that Donald's motor launch is out of order. He's still waiting for parts from Barrow, and he doesn't expect to get them now till the bad weather is over.'

'And the good news?'

'He has a catboat, the *Tigger*. Donald is a great Winnie-the-Pooh fan. The boat has room for three people. It could do the trick, if you think you can sail it.'

I nodded.

'I know his boat quite well. Where is it?'

'That's the other good news. He's moored it at the steamer jetty while the steamers are down at the other end of the lake.'

Rose took my hand.

'You'll both have to keep warm. There'll be a sharp wind on the lake, and it could be dangerous if you get a chill. How will you get back?'

'On the boat, of course. It's about four miles each way.'

She shook her head, and Jeanie and Dr Raverat followed suit.

'My medical advice is that you shouldn't do this at all. For one thing, you're under enormous stress following Octavia's death, and for another you must be exhausted. It's after one o'clock, and I know I'm tired.'

'I need to do it tonight,' I said. 'You heard the weather fore-cast earlier. If we wait till morning, the lake may freeze over and the roads will be more impassable than ever.

Oliver broke in.

'The snow I brought in with me was the last, for now. All the cloud is breaking up and it's going to get a lot colder. But if the cloud is blown away, there'll be a good wind and the moon's a week past the half turn.'

'Have it your way, but I can't come with you. I have patients who may need me. Rose and I will carry Octavia to the boat.'

Oliver was right. The moon wasn't at its best, but it was bright and getting brighter. Everywhere, stars had emerged, as if to welcome my sister into their silent world. Rose and the doctor placed her on deck, facing towards the stern, with some room to spare. A catboat has a gaff-rigged mast set far forward, and a single sail. The beam's very broad, leaving room on deck. Oliver and I had to stay there in order to navigate. He was not a sailor, which put the greatest burden on me.

We were well supplied for our eight-mile journey, down and back. In addition to our coats and hats and scarves and gloves, Jeanie filled the *Tigger* with heaps of blankets, stone hot-water bottles and two flasks of hot soup.

I hugged Rose goodbye, and her mother, and shook the doctor's hand. He was still concerned, but he knew there was nothing more he could do.

Donald McIntyre was at the jetty, of course. He told me how sorry he was to hear of Octavia's death. He said he'd watched her on her walks through the village and been entranced by her pale, childlike beauty.

He came on board with me and spent ten minutes reminding me how to sail a catboat.

'I brought this over from the States,' he told me. 'They sail a lot of them there. You'll be running before the wind all the way to Howtown. Take care of the boom, in case it flies off from one side of the boat to the other, and be careful of swamping. There are heavy waves tonight, and this boat will wallow if you're not very careful.'

And so we sailed out into the lake and into the darkness. Sailing was difficult at first, and for a while we took on water, which Oliver threw back out again. But finally I was able to take control at the helm, keeping us on course by careful turns of the rudder.

For a while Oliver and I talked. He asked how things went with my parents in London.

'Not well at all,' I said. 'My father says he will disown me if I marry Rose.'

He was surprised, and I told him things about my father I had never told anyone. He listened well, and he avoided counselling me, as he might well have done to a regular parishioner. I asked him why he had never married, for I guessed him to be well over thirty.

'I wasn't lucky like you,' he said. 'I didn't meet the right woman.'

'It's not too late. I suspect it's never too late. My mother-in-law-to-be has you in her sights, you know. Not for herself, but for any number of young women she thinks would make good vicars' wives. She says a vicar without a wife is only half a vicar and half a man.'

'Well, she's right there. A wife and family are important assets in our trade. Some say the mission fields are the place to go hunting.'

I laughed.

'You don't need to travel that far. I went to Dakar and lost my leg and found a wife back at home.'

In the end, we had to concentrate so much on navigating and keeping warm that a silence fell on us. I looked up at the great expanse of the night sky. Even in its half light, the moon as it moved cast a blue-white glow on countless galaxies, and the stars moved too. If I had believed in angels, I might have seen them striding across the bright pinnacles of the stars, their wings lambent with starlight. I remembered that Octavia had always loved the angels on our Christmas cards and the angel figures in our nativity. And who am I to say I do not believe in angels, when I have spoken with ghosts and seen their pale faces in a dark room, while Octavia looked on?

I lay back, watching it all, and there was silence across the lake. I thought it ironic that Octavia, who had spent her short life in an aching silence should make this, her final journey, through the greatest silence one can imagine. She lay at my feet in a white sheet like a shroud, and I knew that if I touched her she would be colder than death itself. But I could not bear to think of that, so continued to look up at the stars.

It was not easy navigating at night, and had it not been for the moon and the starlight, we should surely have lost our bearings completely. We hugged the eastern shoreline, passing Sharrow Bay, while the fells loomed over us like giants in the night sky.

Suddenly we saw yellow lights that flickered on the moving water ahead. At first, neither of us could make out what they were, but as we drew near it hit me like a blow that they were coming from the windows of Hallinhag House. I wanted to stop, but as I prepared to do so, the body in the sheet began to move.

'She's still alive!' I shouted. 'Dr Raverat must have made a mistake.'

Oliver put his hand on my arm. Octavia moved again, and when she tried to speak, her voice was muffled by the sheet.

'No, Dominic, this isn't Octavia. Octavia is dead, you must believe that. When we get her to the church, you'll see for yourself. Her body is in the grip of that evil place. Leave her and pray for her. Let me pray for her, but don't let them win.'

'We have to go back there.'

'But not with Octavia. That's not where she belongs. You know that as well as I do. Let me bury her in the graveyard at St Martin's. Some of her ancestors are buried there already. She belongs there.'

And so we sailed past, and once we had left the house behind, the writhing of the thing on the deck became still and I no longer believed she was alive.

We steered to the little landing at Martindale, and when we had tied up, we lifted her in wet sheets and carried her to the church. Our breath hung on the moonlight like cream, and my eyes were wet with tears. Oliver found a little catafalque in the vestry, and together we laid her in the nave, head towards the altar, surrounded by saints and cherubs. He found a couple of albs, also in the vestry, and we removed the soaking nightdress and sheets, dried her with towels and clothed her in the albs.

We debated what to do next. I was loathe to leave Octavia here alone in order to sail back to Pooley Bridge, and even the vicarage seemed too far from her. I realized that the funeral would have to be my parents' decision, and I knew I would soon have to ring them. But that would have to wait until the morning. Oliver brought out some Aladdin heaters, and we sat in front of them. When we had warmed ourselves a little, Oliver suggested we use a pew each to sleep on. I was so tired by then that I made an effort, placing hassocks underneath me for some comfort. It was not the best night's sleep I have ever had, but it saw me through to morning.

We woke up aching and cold. As soon as seemed reasonable, we made our way to Pooley Bridge. Birds huddled in the trees, cold and hungry. The little boat took to the water again, like a silver fish.

I was reluctant to go past Hallinhag, but Oliver pointed at the house.

'It's dark again,' he said. 'I think we can go by.'

And so sail on we did, but not without my feeling an intense tightness in my chest and fear running through me like a metal rod that had become red-hot.

It took us over an hour to get to Howtown, and when we came to the village everything seemed closed and the whole place deserted. We went straight to Jeanie's cottage, and while she made Oliver welcome, I was never so relieved to be in Rose's arms again, frost on my eyebrows and ice on my moustache. Then she kissed me, and the ice melted.

Oliver had wanted to go back home too, but Jeanie forced him to take his coat off and sit in front of the fire facing Rose and me. Once there, he promised to stay for the night. He said he would like to bury Octavia on Sunday, just three days away. He said he wanted his parishioners to be there, and any of the refugee children who were still living locally.

'Most of your relations will be stuck in other parts of the country,' he said. 'But I'm anxious about your parents. You should speak to them this evening.'

Cecil was upstairs, working hard on the letters and other papers. I spoke to him briefly, but we were both much preoccupied, so I left him to it.

Dr Raverat turned up shivering and took a seat near the fire. He seemed peaky. But the kitchen was warm, and we crammed ourselves in at the table to drink hot barley and bean soup with slices of homemade bread and butter.

Afterwards, Raverat and I made our way to his house. Rose came with us: she had patients to see to, and we were hardly inside when the doorbell rang, announcing the arrival of the first.

I rang our London number. The operator put me through as

usual, but after several clicks and buzzes it remained dead. The operator came back on and said it was probably the fault of the line at Barrow, which had been giving trouble since the snow-fall. But I asked her to try the office, and gave her the number. A receptionist answered straight away,

'Lancaster Port Importers. Who do you wish to speak to?'

'This is Dominic Lancaster. I'd like to speak to my father, please.'

There was a short pause, then she came back.

'I'm going to put you through to his secretary, Miss Williams.'

'If he's in a meeting, can she pull him out of it? I have important news for him.'

'I'm putting you through to Miss Williams right now.'

There was a click on the line, then a softer ring. Someone picked up the receiver.

'Pauline Williams. May I help you?'

I repeated my name and asked to be put through.

There was a longer pause. When she spoke again, her voice sounded wrong.

'Mr Lancaster, em, are you sitting down?'

'Well, yes. What's wrong?'

'Are you in London, sir?'

'No, I'm up at Ullswater. We have a house up here.'

'That's nice, sir, I'm pleased to hear it. Sir, I have some very bad news for you.'

'That's all right,' I said, 'I was there when she died. I took her to the church, and we'll try to bury her on Sunday.'

Another pause.

'Do you mean your mother, sir? Were you in London last night, is that what you mean, sir?'

'Of course not my mother. My sister Octavia. I'm ringing to let my father know what happened.'

198

'I don't understand, sir. Do you mean your sister was in the flat last night?'

'In the flat?'

'When the bomb fell, sir. Didn't you know? There was a raid last night, and some parts of Bloomsbury were hit. The block your flat was in took a direct hit. Sir, your parents were at home at the time. They're both dead, sir, I'm terribly sorry. And you say your sister is dead as well?'

I put down the phone. Raverat could sense that something was wrong. He came by my side and let me recover. It was not that I loved my father or my mother; but coming so soon on top of Octavia's death, it seemed too much of a bereavement. They would not be missed, not by me, at least, and probably not by many others, but their deaths brought an era to an end and opened up new possibilities and new responsibilities. I wished Octavia were here with me to share them.

We went back to Rose's cottage, where my news was heard with disbelief. Only Rose really knew how much of a weight had been lifted from me. I could be honest with her, but with the others I put on a brave face.

That night, more snow fell stubbornly like feathers from the wings of swans. Without Octavia, the world seemed empty and quieter. The snow fell and our world was deadened. Moonlight and starlight had left us. There would be little sunshine tomorrow. I wept at times for Octavia, and Rose put her arms around me, but I found no sorrow in me for my parents.

'It's not over yet,' I said. Rose nodded.

'Do you think they killed her?'

'Who?'

'The other children. They killed little Jimmy Ashton. I don't think they can be trusted.'

The snow fell. We could not bear to keep the curtains shut

and we would not extinguish a single lamp. But no planes came over that night. The world was snow and ice and silence.

When I took my last look, snow was falling flake by flake on Octavia's grave. It had been the very devil to dig in the first place. The sexton and his mate had been forced to burn fires to melt the frozen ground, and they had to go down several inches before reaching loose soil. Mrs Mather, who took the money for the steamers when they were running and served cream teas for the passengers an hour before embarkation, had found a lovely white dress that had belonged to her daughter Matilda, who had died at the same age as Octavia. Rose dressed her in this, and someone found a ring of silk flowers to place across her forehead. Tom Arberry and his son had carved a little coffin for her, and polished it and painted it white.

The little church was full for the burial service. Oliver read from the *Book of Common Prayer*, and though I was not touched as a believer, the words sank deeply. He read from Psalm Thirty-nine.

LORD, let me know mine end, and the number of my days; that I may be certified how long I have to live.

Behold, thou hast made my days as it were a span long, and mine age is even as nothing in respect of thee . . .

For man walketh in a vain shadow, and disquieteth himself in vain; he heapeth up riches, and cannot tell who shall gather them . . .

For I am a stranger with thee, and a sojourner, as all my fathers were.

*O spare me a little, that I may recover my strength, before I go
hence, and be no more seen.*

Throughout the service Rose held my hand. Everyone else I
knew was there, Rose's mother Dr Raverat. Oliver Braithwaite
and Cecil, who had moved across to the Lakeside Inn. We had
taken a circuitous route to get to the church. Old Jeremiah
Timms, who runs a little coach between Pooley Bridge and
more far-flung parts like Keswick and Penrith, heard of our
predicament and offered us his services free of charge. He said
he would drive us down the opposite bank, where the road is
much better, and take us just a bit further than Aira Force. After
that, we could walk across the lake – which froze over last night
– and back on the eastern shore, we could walk to the church. I
found the going very hard, but I was determined not to make a
fuss. Rose stayed close beside me the whole way and whispered
words of encouragement. I thought the ice would break and
hurl us into the freezing water, but it did not.

It was a long journey back, but we were there well before dark.
I went with Cecil to his hotel room. Waiting for me was a table
full of papers.

'We need to talk, sir,' he said. 'But first, I need to give you
my condolences, again, on your father's death. Well . . . I think
you know better than most that he could be a difficult man. He
was often a tyrant to work for, if you don't mind my saying so.'

'Not at all. Fire away.'

'But he ran the business well and kept us all employed.
Lancaster's is still the finest port house in London. But now he's
gone, all the employees will be wondering what's to happen
next. Especially given the war and shipping and all that. Is it too
early to ask if you have any plans, sir?'

'For the business, you mean?'

'Well, yes sir, if you don't mind my asking, sir.'

'Cecil, stop calling me "sir". I answer to Dominic still like anybody else. The answer to your question is that I don't know for sure. Not yet. I'm planning to get married, and I have to count that in. But there's a very good chance I'll take on the directorship. It's a family business, as you know better than anyone, and I think it would be a shame to break with that tradition. So, for the moment, I'll say it's very likely.'

He smiled with satisfaction, but I wasn't yet prepared to say 'yes' or 'no'. I still had things to do. Scores to settle. Ghosts to lay.

'You will need to get to London as soon as possible, sir. Sorry, Dominic. The business will be in trouble if it's left with no one at the helm.'

'I'll bear that in mind, thank you. Now, what else do you have for me?'

He took me through his research slowly. William had built Hallinhag House, using stone from the quarry in nearby Shap and slate from Stockdalebank Quarry in Longsleddale. And when it was built the ships started to arrive.

'Some sailed as far as Barrow-in-Furness,' he said, 'but most docked in London.'

'Bringing port.'

He shook his head.

'Yes and no. Port shipments then were not very large. Sometimes the ships brought slaves from Portugal, slaves from their colonies in Africa and from Macau in China. That trade continued till the eighteen hundreds. The Chinese were all children. Most were sent on to the Americas, until 1761, when the Portuguese banned the slave trade. But in Brazil the trade continued until the 1880s at the rate of sixty thousand slaves a year.

I think our children were in close contact with slaves, here or back in Portugal, or both. Here's a letter from William that mentions them:

> The children play a game they call Maculell. It is a dance
> performed with sticks, that bears great similarity to our country
> Morris dances, but the children say they were taught this dance
> for entertainment by a black slave they knew in Portugal. And
> they do not always dance themselves, but use fome rag dolls with
> their features painted black, like they were black fellows from the
> Africas or the Brazils. They hold the dolls and speak to them as
> they speak to thofe others, and fometimes they do paint their own
> faces, as it were in a masque. And then they do sometimes dance
> on their bare feet, and the sound of their bal mafqué, with the
> clacking of sticks and the beating of their feet comes down from
> the attic loud enough to awaken the dead.

'Sir, the dance is called *maculelé*. It is still danced by the descendants of the African slaves in Brazil.'

'Dominic, please.'

I told him about the dancing children I had seen in the house, their stamping feet and twirling and beating of sticks.

'And is that it?' I asked.

'Not quite. You say you smelled something like bodies of the dead in Hallinhag House?

'Yes, on one evening in particular.'

'Let me explain to you what they brought in with the port. William imported corpses, mostly nailed up inside casks that had been used for port. No customs inspector ever asked a question. The corpses came from contacts of his around Europe, from France, Portugal and Spain, and they were transported to Ullswater. I believe they were kept in the attic, and that

203

the children lived with them. Some were mummified, others trussed up in burlap sacks. Others came from friends of William's in Britain.'

'I don't understand,' I said, with horror. 'Why would anyone collect corpses? I just can't see the point of it.'

'They were for the children. The children spoke to them and asked questions, and the corpses answered, answers from beyond the grave. It was a power the children had or had been taught. They were "ghost talkers": that's what William calls them. His Portuguese correspondents call them much the same: *faladores de fantasmas*. The dead would speak, and those who had reason would write down questions for the children. "Where is the gold, where are my mother's jewels, where did you put your last will and testament?" What's more, it worked. Secrets were revealed that could have come from no other source. Some of William's circle wanted more, of course. The mysteries of the universe, the secrets of the human soul. They had disinterred bodies belonging to philosophers, poets and even saints. Either the children couldn't handle that sort of material or ghosts know no more than we do and refused to answer.'

'And you think these mummies were kept in an attic at Hallinhag.'

'There's no doubt about the attic, Dominic, and there's no doubt that it was boxed in at some point. We just have to use the architect's drawings I found earlier and work out how to get at the attic.'

'We'll start in the morning,' I said. 'I'll find some builders.'

Cecil shook his head.

'Not a good idea. If they find anything, word of it will be round Howtown and Pooley Bridge in an hour, and in Keswick and Penrith in another, and before you know it the local press will force their way in with cameras and sharp-nosed reporters.

204

Then it will be on the radio. Dominic, while the war is on, the press are desperate for domestic stories. This would keep them going for weeks. It's not good for the business, or your future family.'

'Then what do you suggest?'

'Get us all together, you, me, the doc and the minister. It shouldn't be hard work, trust me.'

'The morning, then. We'll do it together.'

Monday, 13 January

Waking the next morning, we found that the temperature had risen a little and the lake had shed its ice. We – Rose, myself, Dr Raverat, Cecil and the Reverend Braithwaite – all piled into the two cars belonging to the doctor and the vicar and set off south along the lake's edge. We knew we were taking a risk, since the road was still much covered in snow and slippery with ice. We went equipped with crowbars, hammers and an axe I found in Jeanie's shed. She asked no questions about the nature of our expedition.

We arrived outside the house without mishap. No lamps were lit, but the front door was open. I pushed it back further, and we could see that snow had blown into the wide hallway and icicles had formed everywhere.

We all got inside and I closed the door. It fell to with a heavy bang. I shivered, grateful for the light that came through the windows. It was all familiar, yet unfamiliar. Things had happened here that I will never forget so long as I live.

We were all waiting for something. A sound, the image of a dead child, dancing slaves, the beating of a drum, voices,

205

whispers, the high voices of children caught between death and the end of death, fear creeping across the floor on muffled feet, a pounding of feet on the stairs, cold creeping round our necks like a noose of ice, eyes in the darkness looking at us without compassion or guilt, the cold hands of ghost talkers, their whispers and the whispers of their dead . . .

I opened the door of the dining room. No one was there. But on the table I noticed a jigsaw of Octavia's. When we had last been here, the puzzle had been half-finished. Now it was complete.

'Octavia?' I asked. 'Are you here?'

Nothing. A perfect silence. Rose took me away. I was clumsy on my leg.

'My leg,' I said. 'It hurts like hell.'

'Yes, I know,' she replied. 'I'll look at it once we're done. Dr Raverat's here. He can give you some morphia. Is it bad enough for that?'

I nodded, and Raverat came with his bag and his needle and a smile on his face as he injected me. Minutes passed and the pain was gone, but I felt a little groggy. Rose kissed my forehead. Her face spun for a moment, then cleared. She took my hand. The others were standing in the doorway.

We went all through the ground floor. Apart from the bitter cold, all was just as it had been.

We headed for the stairs. The treads creaked, and I heard whispers above my head. The doctor went first, then Oliver and Cecil. Rose and I came last.

As we got to the top, I started to feel dizzy. The morphia was making me feel drowsy. There was a chair on the landing. I sat down and felt myself spin off into a half-dreaming half-awake state, and as I did so I could see dancing figures in a haze, their faces blackened as before, turning in the dance like rag dolls with wooden hands and wooden feet and eyes that were always turned towards me. They danced in my direction but never came any closer. I shouted at them to go back, but they kept on coming without ever reaching me.

Then the dancing men grew smaller and smaller and faded, and when I came to Rose was kneeling beside me, holding my hand and whispering softly in my ear. Dr Raverat was there.

'I think we've got to get you back home,' he said. 'The rest of us can manage here. Oliver will drive you back.'

I shook my head.

'I won't go back till I've seen what's up here. It was just too much morphia. It has happened before, Rose can tell you. I'll be fine.'

Raverat seemed sceptical, but he looked at my eyes with the help of a tiny torch he always carried.

'Very well, but please be careful. If there are any shocks, tell Rose or one of us to get you down and outside.'

Rose helped me round, and I soon gained strength. The top floor was as I remembered it from my earlier stays. Bedrooms ready for occupation, a large bathroom and toilet, some cupboards, five electric heaters. The bedrooms contained beds that were all in serious need of an airing. There were photographs on the bedside tables, and oil lamps, and paintings on the wall showing the first signs of damp.

Without the drawings, we should have been forced to tear down most of the walls in order to find a way into the attic space, but they showed very clearly where the attics had been. We focused on a broad expanse of wall next to the master bedroom. If the drawing was right, this would be where the stairs had been. Very old wallpaper in a pattern of Chinese birds ran across this entire section. We scraped it off and found planking underneath. It was simply a matter of using the crowbars and hammers to pull back the planks. With two or three out of the way, I was able to put a torch into the space. Right behind it lay a short flight of wooden steps, exactly as we had anticipated. We forced the other planks from the horizontal struts on to which they had been nailed. The struts themselves came away easily. It had fallen completely silent. I could hear nothing but the sound of my own breathing. I realized I was sweating in spite of the cold. With one hand I loosened my scarf. Then I shone my torch onto the steep stairwell. Oliver and Dr Raverat switched on their torches as well. All along and above the stairs was a wash of cobwebs, but there were few spiders among them. The space had been shut off for a very long time, and I could not think how spiders might have survived there without prey to feed on.

Rose had found a witch's broom downstairs and used it now to clear the stairway. We went up slowly, one stair at a time, and in a very short time I found myself face to face with a wooden door. It was grimy. In front of me was a handwritten inscription bearing a single word. I read it out letter by letter while Cecil wrote it down. I guessed it was Portuguese. The word was *Aleijadinhos*.

'I came across this in several letters from Sir William,' Cecil said. 'Literally, it means "little cripples", but somehow it became a sort of slang for lepers. The formal word would be *leprosos* nowadays, but *aleijadinho* was current in William's day.'

A crowbar took care of the lock, which swung away from us. We stepped inside, one at a time. As I came through the door, I felt lightheaded again. But I knew I was at the heart of this thing. I took a step forward and let the beam of my torch go all the way to the other end of the attic. I heard a tapping, like the feet of tap dancers or Irish dancers. But this was more staccato. It would break off for long moments, then resume, then stop again. As my torch travelled round the long room, I saw

208

something. I halted the torch and looked more closely, and my heart almost gave out. I heard Rose gasp with horror, then the doctor, then Oliver and Cecil.

Everywhere I looked was a tumble of coffins and corpses, some mummified, some skeletons, many clothed in mouldering habits, the treasure trove of one man's obsession with the dreams of the dead, the febrile nightmares of the departed. They filled the attic. Some corpses sat on chairs, wisps of hair on their bald pates, their jaws fallen, others lay half in, half out of their coffins, yet others had been wrapped in burlap and tied up with string.

I noticed an array of four mummified bodies dressed in eighteenth-century clothes, and in the same moment I realized they were no bigger than children. I looked more closely and saw that one was dressed in the grave clothes that had appeared in Rose's photograph of Clara. Three had long hair, the fourth was almost bald, and only one wore boy's clothes. Four dolls with black faces lay next to them. Rose squeezed my hand so hard her nails dug into my palm.

I had expected to see the children themselves, or other figures raised by the ghost talkers out of their own sleep, but none appeared. I was horrified by the possibility that Octavia's spirit could be here, condemned to lie in this long room with the other lepers. The children perhaps.

Just as I thought we should turn and board this charnel-house up again, something moved at the far end. I strained to see, and slowly a figure came into view, a phantom illuminated by the light of my torch.

It was a man in eighteenth-century clothes. He wore a black justaucorps, a gilet, also black, a lawn cravat in the Steenkerk fashion, a bourse wig tied back with a black ribbon, a small black tricorne hat and black shoes with low heels and silver buckles. The very height of fashion, or so it seemed to me. He carried a thin-bladed sword at his waist and a silver-topped cane in his right hand. I could have recognized him anywhere.

He looked at me appraisingly, standing cocksure and arrogant in front of me.

'You must be Sir Dominic,' he said. 'I am Sir William Lancaster, your many times grandfather. Have you found what you were looking for here, or is this all a disappointment? Do tell me. I'd love to have a short conversation. I fear you've grown disillusioned with me. You think this was evil. You believe I am to be reprimanded on account of what has happened here. But these are mere mortal remains. You will find the like in any country churchyard or in the crypt of any large church or cathedral. No one pays them heed. No one gives them gratuitous attention. Yet some are murderers, some have been brought to the hangman's noose, others to the executioner's sword, some innocent yet put to death, others steeped in sin and properly hanged and quartered. You say nothing of those, yet here you protest that something evil has been done. Fie on you for a mawkish, condoling buffoon.'

I said nothing. What can one say to the dead? He was the picture of elegance, a doyen of wit, and clearly my father's predecessor, yet underneath he was but a rotting carcass, and beneath that he had a heart as black and unfeeling as any you might hope to find with Adolf Hitler and his circle of the damned. I had always boasted that I did not believe in hell, but now I hoped for it, hoped that William Lancaster and his associates might tumble into its deepest pit. And then I guessed that they might be in hell already. I could almost smell the faggots burning.

I called to the others, and I could see they were as eager as I was to get out of there. They joined me, and we locked the door, shutting the attic away from sight. We hurried back down the stairway, bunched together. I told them what I wanted to do

210

and, though reluctant, they helped me nail the boards back in place. They went back firmly, and when we had finished it was hard to see any difference from the way the wall was now and how it was when we arrived. All it needed was some wallpaper to turn it back to what was there before.

It was silent behind the wall and door. A perfect silence had fallen on the house, a silence of ghosts quiet as the corpses in their graves, as quiet as the bones in the attic. The silence of ghosts. With each other they never talk, they never sing. With the living, they whisper in our ears and scream in our heads.

We left and the cold air licked at our wounds. There was nothing more I could do. I no longer had the strength, my thoughts could take no more of it. I needed to think of Rose and the life I would live with her.

Saturday, 10 May

There have been large air raids on Barrow for several days now. The German planes pass over the lakes, and the booming of their engines puts fear into all our hearts. There's a special service in the church tomorrow, to pray for our neighbours over there and to remember the many who have died. We dare not show a light now, for fear an over-hasty German bomber gets it into his head and presses the button to send a torrent of Sprengbrand C50 incendiaries on top of Pooley Bridge. It will soon be time to leave Ullswater and return to London.

Rose and I were married last Sunday, on a gloriously sunny day. We had guests from Pooley Bridge, Howtown and beyond, and there was barely enough room in the church for everyone. Oliver Braithwaite married us, as we had asked him to, and

211

Hugh Raverat gave Rose away. Jeanie sat in the front pew and cried her eyes out, as is only natural. That same day, Jeanie went off on a holiday, to stay with relatives in Keswick, who took her there in their car.

She left us her cottage to stay in for our honeymoon, and we've barely set foot outside. The baker leaves a loaf of bread, the dairy farmer bottles of milk, and the grocer everything else we need. We just leave our ration books on the doorstep, and a basket for the groceries. We are in perfect heaven.

And when we're in bed and I run my hands along her naked back, I feel nothing but her skin. The fear has gone.

We have done what we can down at Hallinhag House. Oliver Braithwaite said prayers for all those who had died, nameless and faceless, before being left in that attic of horrors. I have done with the house now and will leave it to return to the silence I found it in.

Octavia's tombstone was made of local granite and inscribed by a stonemason from Penrith. She sleeps in silence now, like those other dead. I no longer dream of dancing men and I do not hear the stamping of children's feet as they dance the *maculelé*. Hallinhag House sits where it has been for centuries, its rooms empty, its windows unpolished, shunned by young and old. The people of Howtown know only that it has a bad reputation. But some of us know better.

Afterword by Charles Lancaster

So, it falls to me to have the last word. What sort of inheritance will I leave to my children? A truncated history of their ancestors and their doings? Images of our family's graves, a rattling of Lancaster bones shaken by our living hands in their sealed sarcophagi or little ossuaries. Shall I leave them a house that is haunted, shall I bring them into the company of ghosts, remind them that the dead can speak, the dead can scream, the dead can kill?

Little William is five, his sister Octavia is twice his age, somewhere around the age Dominic's sister had reached when she died. He had told me her name and that she had been profoundly deaf and that she had died young. To me, my children are immortal. I talked to Jess about it yesterday. She agrees. We both know that our children will die one day, but we are confident that neither of us will still be alive when that moment comes. Of course, we may be wrong. There are accidents, diseases, unlawful killings, attacks by wild animals, drownings, fire and all the many incidents to which we humans are always exposed. We pray not, and every night we watch over them.

I met Octavia again three weeks ago, when I went to Hallinhag. For the last time, perhaps.

'Do you know who I am?' I asked, and I was trembling because I knew all too well who she was and what she was.

She nodded. 'You must be my brother's grandson. You are one of us. One of the family.'

'Dominic and Rose were my grandparents. Rose died a few years ago, and Dominic after her.'

'I know,' she said. 'I've seen them here. They look quite young again.'

'Really? That must be nice for them, after all these years.'

She shook her head slowly, side to side. 'I don't think they like it here,' she said, not like a child speaking at all. 'They never liked this house. Too many bodies, too many voices.'

'But you can hear now? And speak!'

She nodded and her face lit up. 'Of course,' she said. 'I'm a ghost talker now, you see. I have my friends. I taught them English and they taught me Portuguese. Have you come to tear Hallinhag House down? If you do, we'll all have to leave.'

I shook my head. 'No,' I said, 'I would never do that. I have too many plans. I will take some of the gardens away, that's all. Perhaps you can point out which is which. I want to bring my own dead here, and you and your friends can ask them questions and tell me what they say. Will you be content with that?'

'Why don't you come inside and speak with the other children?'

And she smiled and opened the door for me and led me inside.

Her body is in the churchyard and the daffodils that were planted long ago on her grave are blooming. I am sure her soul is at rest. For the moment.

The vicar at Martindale is the grandson of Dominic's Oliver Braithwaite. Oliver found his wife in the end, without going out into the missionary field. I gave him the diaries to read, and when he finished them he agreed something had to be done. With the help of his two sextons, we transferred the bones, all the contents of the coffins, from the attic to a large plot at the back of the graveyard. The Reverend Braithwaite and I shook hands. And I got in touch with a local firm of builders. They finished work last week, and the house is inhabitable again.

Charles Lancaster's personal diary

Sir William remains. He seems happy with what I have suggested. The four children will remain too, as ghost talkers. And Octavia. They will be jewels in our midst, the keys to ten thousand secrets.

I wrote and posted a letter yesterday

My Lord, the Earl Dunlop
I believe your ancestor, Earl Howard, was well acquainted with
my own ancestor, Sir William Lancaster. If you would care to
meet me, I can relate what I know about the connection they
forged. I have in my possession a number of letters sent to and
from Earl Howard and my ancestor, and I suspect that, if you
have an archive, you will find letters there also. I will bring with
me a proposal that I believe will prove to be of mutual benefit.

Let me know your feelings on this meeting and, if you will, an
early date, either at my place in Bedford Square or at yours. You
are not, of course, so very far away.
Yours sincerely,
Sir Charles Lancaster